GOBLIN SLAYER

SIDE STORY: YEAR ONE

2

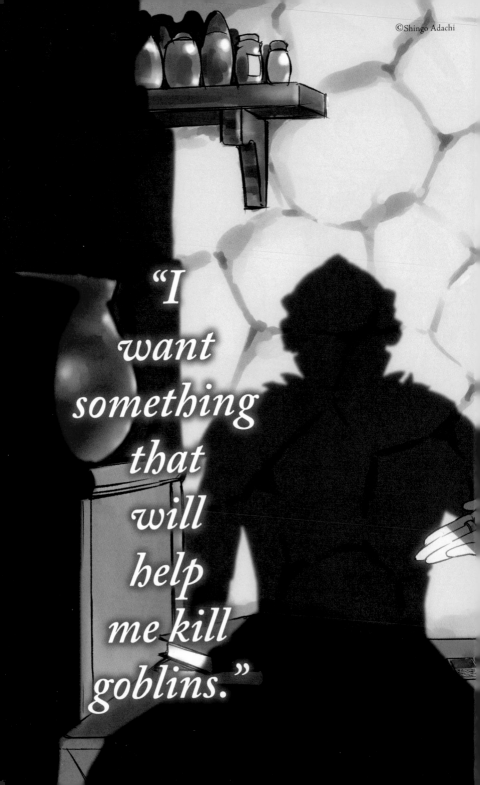

Contents

GOBLIN SLAYER

SIDE STORY: YEAR ONE

©Shingo Adachi

GOBLIN SLAYER

SIDE STORY: YEAR ONE

VOLUME 2

KUMO KAGYU

Illustration by
SHINGO ADACHI

YEN ON

New York

GOBLIN SLAYER

SIDE STORY: YEAR ONE

❦ VOLUME 2 ❧

KUMO KAGYU

Translation by Kevin Steinbach ❧ Cover art by Shingo Adachi

GOBLIN SLAYER GAIDEN: YEAR ONE volume 2
Copyright © 2018 Kumo Kagyu
Illustrations copyright © 2018 Shingo Adachi
All rights reserved.
Original Japanese edition published in 2018 by SB Creative Corp.
This English edition is published by arrangement with SB Creative Corp., Tokyo in care of Tuttle-Mori Agency, Inc., Tokyo.

English translation © 2019 by Yen Press, LLC

Yen On
150 West 30th Street, 19th Floor
New York, NY 10001

Visit us at yenpress.com ✿ facebook.com/yenpress ✿ twitter.com/yenpress ✿ yenpress.tumblr.com ✿ instagram.com/yenpress

First Yen On Edition: July 2019

Yen On is an imprint of Yen Press, LLC.
The Yen On name and logo are trademarks of Yen Press, LLC.

The publisher is not responsible for websites (or their content) that are not owned by the publisher.

Library of Congress Cataloging-in-Publication Data
Names: Kagyū, Kumo, author. | Adachi, Shingo, illustrator. | Steinbach, Kevin, translator.
Title: Goblin Slayer side story year one / Kagyu Kumo ; illustration by Shingo Adachi ; translation by Kevin Steinbach.
Other titles: Goblin Slayer gaiden year one. English
Description: First Yen On edition. | New York : Yen On, 2018–
Identifiers: LCCN 2018027845 | ISBN 9781975302849 (v. 1 : pbk.) | ISBN 9781975357634 (v. 2 : pbk.)
Subjects: LCSH: Goblins—Fiction. | GSAFD: Fantasy fiction.
Classification: LCC PL872.5.A367 G5613 2018 | DDC 895.63/6—dc23
LC record available at https://lccn.loc.gov/2018027845

ISBNs: 978-1-9753-5763-4 (paperback)
        978-1-9753-3177-1 (ebook)

10 9 8 7 6 5 4 3 2 1

LSC-C

Printed in the United States of America

GOBLIN SLAYER

SIDE STORY: YEAR ONE

❖ VOLUME 2 ❖

Gods, Gods!
Roll the dice and play a game.
Roll a one and I'll comfort you,
roll a two and I'll laugh with you,
roll a three and I'll praise you,
roll a four and I'll give you a treat,
roll a five and I'll dance for you,
roll a six and I'll kiss you,
roll a seven and it's off the board.

CHAPTER 1

AFTER SESSION, SCENARIO HOOK
The End of One Fight, the Shadow of Another

The crimson-stained earth grew darker as it caught the colors of twilight. The wind that whipped over the wasteland blew cold and carried with it the smells of death and rust, and air scorched by magic.

Gods, what greed.

The monk crouched by a few spears that had been stuck in the ground to stop horses, examining his surroundings nonchalantly. The field had been ringing with the cacophony of combat not long before, but now all was silent—the clash of swords, the whinnying of horses, incantations and war cries, death rattles... When the last sounds of the battle's pomp and circumstance had faded away, only a pervading loneliness remained.

The monk found that truly disturbing.

"Master Monk, there you are."

The voice came as a surprise, though the footsteps had reached his ears.

The general had dull golden hair tied up, and although her knight's armor was old, she herself was young. She was responsible for one of the little fortresses here on the frontier and commanded a motley collection of soldiers and mercenaries.

At the moment, she was leaning on her slender sword as if it were a walking staff; but even now the monk could still see her swinging the weapon from horseback. He'd heard she was of noble stock, and he believed the strength she'd shown would have made her ancestors proud.

"You've turned out to be quite lovely," he said.

"...Is that sarcasm?"

"Humor is one of my many talents, but I would never use it in regards to a woman's looks."

The general blinked her right eye in confusion.

The other eye was missing from her striking face; from her elegant body, an arm and a leg had been torn off. Her perfect form, blemished. The result of her intensity in battle, or perhaps its cost.

Her bandages were caked in drying black streaks of blood, and her breath came shallow and painful.

Still, she had acquitted herself in combat; she had survived and was still here. If that was not beautiful, what was?

The general frowned in the scarlet of twilight, then coughed once. "Gathering up the bodies took time. I'm sorry you had to wait. Can you handle the funeral?"

"But of course, of course."

The young monk got to his feet, looking almost lighthearted. Flecks of blood spattered his garments, but he seemed to pay them no mind.

"How would you prefer the memorial to be done?"

"What do you do in your sect?"

"Our faith teaches that if the corpse is exposed and returned to creation, it will one day be reborn as someone stronger."

"You mean... Respawn?" She frowned as if the word was unfamiliar, or at least unpleasant. "...We dug a hole and tossed the enemy bodies in. I want you to say the prayers when we set them alight."

"Certainly, certainly."

The monk matched the general's pace as they approached the earthworks lined with spears. An enemy cavalry charge had left some of the shafts broken, like a mouth missing teeth. As they walked through the uneven mass of shadows, the monk said, as casually as if he were discussing the weather, "They say those who don't fit their niche are doomed to die... Heh-heh."

"I don't necessarily have anything against your kind, monk. One of you even visited my home once, long ago."

My little sister rather took to him.

That provoked an "Oh-ho" from the monk. Then he asked, "And what of the goblins? There were many on the field today. Would you see them given rites as well?"

"Yes, I'm afraid," the general said tiredly. "Goblins or not, we can't have them turning undead on us."

They were heading for a corner of the wasteland that seemed as dark as if a pot of ink had been spilled upon it.

It was the pit into which the bodies had been thrown. All of them monsters—Non-Prayer Characters. With the exception of the likes of dark elves, Non-Prayer Characters never carried off the bodies of their dead. This was because they expected that through a hex, they would become ghosts and return to fight once more.

It was Pray-ers alone who retrieved the corpses of their companions. Some dismissed this practice as nothing more than pointless sentiment—but no person could live without sentiment.

One was not supposed to have likes and dislikes, the monk reflected. Yet, the moment of an undead ghost's destruction was one of great excitement for him.

With this thought in his mind, he looked down into a trough positively piled with hideous little bodies.

"The foot soldiers of Chaos are certainly plentiful," he said.

"Yeah," the general replied. "And here I thought... I thought the Demon Lord was supposed to have been defeated five years ago." There was just a hint of exhaustion in her sigh. "You know, sometimes...sometimes, I think it must be easy, simply living life hating anything that isn't convenient for you."

The monk couldn't be sure whether she meant mentally easy, or physically. Neither was a subject the monk felt like pursuing. They were staring into a grave full of demons, evil nagas, mutated insects, ghosts, and goblins. He guessed the woman would be just as happy talking about military matters instead.

"Are you still hunting down the stragglers?" he asked, changing the subject.

"We've found some of them. Though I'm hearing there are still periodic goblin attacks to the west."

"The west…" The monk turned his eyes to the horizon and the last light of the setting sun. Behind him, the deep blue of eventide had seeped into the sky, which was colored by only the faintest rays of sun. The stars would be out shortly, and the twin moons would begin to reveal their hazy light.

"I've got no interest in being an adventurer. I don't have much education. Hate farming, and I'm sure as hell not going to sell myself. How long is the path between someone like that and simple banditry?"

"Heh-heh. Surely it is well and good for each to find their own niche in which to live."

"I guess at least I found it on my own, even if it was a struggle. Better than being coddled and given everything on a platter…" There was a faint smile on the woman's face, then she grimaced with pain. The monk glanced at her.

"You know of some such as this?"

"The type who think it strange not to be taught how to do things safely or thoroughly even if they never say a word, you know.

"Almost like they think it's really worth that much to go that far for them," she whispered. The monk could not imagine what memories must have prompted her words.

"I don't want people thinking I'm like them," the woman said, "so I came here."

Probably my sister, too.

She looked into the distance, far over the ruined field, and her eyes reflected the horizon. She must have walked through life always seeking a place where she could live.

The monk lifted his chin and, as if to affirm her journey, pronounced, "The world will grow yet more disordered."

"Yes, and isn't that a wonderful thing?"

"Indeed it is, yes, indeed."

The two of them looked at each other, then burst out laughing.

Peace and harmony were fine things. They would never go out of their way to destroy them.

But they had discovered that in battle, they were alive.

Whatsoever the armies of Chaos might throw at them, they would face it head-on and slaughter it.

They had free will, could determine their own actions.

That was the one absolute right they had, even as pawns, that could not be taken from them by the dice of Fate or Chance.

Whatever lay at the end of the path they chose, so long as it was a choice they made, it would lead to the gods' blessing.

Besides, the general's beauty would surely bloom better in the fertile field of battle than secreted away in some plot in the capital. The monk would have hated to see her plucked by some creature with no appreciation for her, and he was overjoyed that she had not chosen that path.

Though he and the female general had simply happened to be walking the same way through life for a brief time, he nonetheless wished her happiness on the road ahead.

"Perhaps we should begin the ceremony, then. Whether buried or burned, all life returns to dust." The monk started veritably gliding down the slope.

The general, looking down at him, asked offhandedly, "Master Monk, where do you intend to go with this battle over?"

"Well now, let's see. My journey merely takes me where the wind blows and in whichever direction my feet carry me, but…" He looked toward the sun as he went. There was hardly so much as a glimmer coming from it anymore, only a thin ray of light lining the horizon. To him, it seemed like a tower that stood at the edge of the world, and he judged it good. "I think the western frontier seems likely to provide me with a great deal of excitement."

Then the young lizardman priest rolled his eyes in delight.

"They call it a dungeon crawl, but it's just mapping out an old mine. There probably won't even be any monsters there. How about we get right to it?"

"Wait, hold on," the young warrior blurted, and he regretted speaking almost as soon as he opened his mouth.

They were in the Adventurers Guild late in the morning, after most of the quests had already been claimed. Sunlight slanted in through the windows, revealing all the dust the adventurers had kicked up. The Guild tried hard to keep the place clean, but with so many visitors wearing so many dusty boots, it was a losing battle.

The warrior could smell the dust in the air with each breath he took. "…I mean, uh… You know," he said, scratching his head. He was apparently trying to make an excuse for something.

Four pairs of eyes stared back at him blankly (or perhaps, wondering what in the world he was thinking). A closer look revealed that everyone staring was even less experienced than the warrior—in fact, they looked like they had just arrived at the Guild that very day. Their equipment was cheap but unblemished, brand-new. And their eyes sparkled.

The girl who stood at the front of their group, her long silver hair tied in a ponytail, looked most earnest of all. She was human, tall, well-endowed, with long legs and toned muscles that suggested she was a martial artist.

But her eyes—they reminded him too much of someone else, and the young warrior could barely get the words out of his mouth.

"They… They don't know if there are monsters down there. That's why they need someone to investigate, right?" He swallowed, then added, "Ambush is always a possibility. It's better to be careful."

"Huh? Oh, uh, right. You're right." Flustered, the silver-haired martial artist turned to her companions. It was obvious the idea hadn't even occurred to them. He could see that not one of the men or women was wearing a helmet, or even carrying a shield.

And they're going to go out and be adventurers.

It was only because he had been on several adventures himself that he understood. He had been so helpless, so immature, so foolish. He saw what an immense difference just a few hours' experience could make.

They didn't know. Didn't realize what unimaginable dangers lurked out there. All they had was the belief that they could hack their way out of any situation with their own strength.

"What do we do…?"

"We can't turn this down. We hardly have any money."

"That's why I said we should think about going to the sewers…"

"And how long would we have to be there to make enough for four people?"

The rookies' huddle seemed to be going nowhere. Just from listening to their back-and-forth, the warrior was fairly sure that the group would end up dead someplace, a textbook case.

It would have been easy to point and laugh. Nobody would have blamed him for simply walking away and forgetting about them. They had nothing to do with him.

Adventurers had to take responsibility for themselves. No one told them how to live, but the trade-off was that no one would be there to help them when they died.

The one modicum of sympathy in their lives was that the Guild afforded them some social status. Compared to being cast out into the wilderness with nothing…

I'm just the same, aren't I?

A moment later, the young warrior heaved a sigh. When he'd

©Shingo Adachi

started out, he'd been no different from these kids—even now, he was still little more than a greenhorn himself. From that perspective, it was shameful to be patronizing and talk down to them.

If I was just going to get upset about it, I would have been better off not talking to them in the first place.

He scratched his head again and turned on his heel as if to leave. He had been planning a nice, easy quest for this afternoon…

"U-um!"

A voice from behind stopped him in his tracks. He turned around, and there was that earnest gaze.

The silver-haired girl bowed her head, making her ponytail bounce.

"I'm sorry for the trouble. And thank you so much for the advice!"

That wasn't exactly what I intended, though.

The girl jogged back to her friends, her silver hair following her like a tail.

The young warrior heaved a sigh, again.

Moping around forever isn't going to help anyone… I guess.

"…You said you had to map out an old mine?" The young warrior started walking toward the newly minted adventurers. He was already thinking about how to help them make good decisions while still letting them find their own way…

CHAPTER 2

ONE RING, ONE SPARK

That day was as terrible and ugly as any other.

The mossy stone ruins were bone-chillingly cold to the touch; sunlight pierced like a needle through a crack in the ceiling.

The goblin on guard duty had a rusty spear in his hand. He gave the floor an irritable kick.

"GOROOBB! GORB!!"

"Eee—yaaaaggghh?! Huurrgh, haaaaghhh!"

"GOROORBB!!"

If he listened carefully enough, he could hear the sounds of merriment coming from the main hall.

Argh—why did he have to get the "night" shift now of all times?

Who would even be stupid enough to come to a place like this?

The goblin had already managed to forget that the people they had caught the other day had been adventurer-explorers. All he remembered was that there had been several men, several women, and the prospect of enjoyment for some time to come. Plus, the dwarf man was plenty fat, so food wouldn't be a concern for a while. The meat was tough, but he wouldn't ask for too much (despite believing that he was naturally entitled to ask for as much as he wanted).

"Hrrrraaaagghhhh?!"

"GBOR!!"

The woman today certainly had a set of lungs on her, though. The goblin licked his lips; they must have come up with a new way to play.

At the beginning, stabbing the heads of the dead men had made the women clamor and shout, which had been quite a lot of fun. But their responses got less emphatic every day, and now they were in danger of becoming downright boring.

Even showing them the heads—thoroughly rotted by now—provoked only a dull "ugh" or "ahh."

But listening to her now, they had to be doing something interesting.

The thought caused the goblin to stamp his feet, making it impossible to stay where he was.

Maybe he could just let guard duty take care of itself?

The goblin nodded; a fine idea, if he did say so himself. No one would notice if he quietly sneaked in to join them. The others should be pulling some guard duty anyway.

Yes, that was what he would do. The goblin threw aside his spear, adjusted his loincloth (it didn't cover much), and turned back.

The next second, he found something wrapped around his mouth, like a snake, and then a sharp blade ran across his throat. The goblin heard the whistling gurgle of his own blood, instants before he began to choke on it.

A moment after that, he was unable to move, and then he was dead.

No one mourned him.

§

"One."

The adventurer kept the twitching goblin's mouth covered until he was sure the creature was no longer breathing, then he slowly rolled the corpse over. He gave his sword a shake to get the blood off, then shoved it back in its scabbard. In its place, he inspected the dropped short spear, then added it to his belt.

There was a limit to how much he could carry, but so long as they didn't become a hindrance, one could never have too many weapons.

Then he silently surveyed the area before kicking the goblin's body into the shadows. Just to be sure.

He took the torch in his left hand and sent it rolling across the floor so that both his hands were empty. Well in the distance, he could hear the unmistakable sounds of goblin revelry.

Slowly, carefully, he brought his heel down, tensing his abdominal muscles so as to be as quiet as possible while he crept along. Trying to sneak along on one's tiptoes used too much energy, and it brought the heaviest part of the body down too quickly. How was anyone supposed to sneak around if they were practically falling all over the place? It was a question his master had posed to him amid a flurry of angry blows.

He spotted a light source, but goblins didn't need light to see by. It was either for warmth, or for fun.

The latter, perhaps.

He was exactly right.

"Ahhh?! Aggghh!"

"GOROBOGO! GOROBOGOGOG!!"

A woman screamed inarticulately, followed by the cackling of goblins. They were taking a metal pole resting in the fire at the center of the room and pressing it to the woman's skin. Each time, she would thrash about trying to escape in a hideous perversion of a dance.

He couldn't tell immediately whether she was an adventurer or a village girl. Terrified and screaming, weeping as she desperately tried to run away, begging for forgiveness, she could have been any girl anywhere. But then there was the jangling of the rank tag around her neck.

She was so thoroughly broken that he couldn't tell who she was, even though they'd given him information prior to the quest. He didn't think about what must have happened to make her this way. He already knew.

And in her own way, she was still better off than the others.

Amid discarded skeletons, he had found several other young women consigned to the blood and muck. Their clouded eyes had lost their light, their bodies were missing things they should have had, and they constantly muttered gibberish to themselves.

Presumably, the remaining prisoners were now in the goblins' stomachs.

Which was the better fate? He didn't bother with the question. He had other things to worry about.

I count four enemies. At least one sword, ax, and club each. No archers. One looks like a hob.

"GOROOBOG! GOROBG!!"

"GBRRG…"

One especially muscular goblin grabbed some meat from a plate (not crafted by the goblins, surely) and took a big bite. Then he gestured with a tug of his chin at another of the goblins, gave the creature a shove, and stole the wine cup from his hand.

Around the big monster's neck sparkled several rank tags he must have taken from adventurers.

This was their leader—it had to be. A hobgoblin.

The adventurer mulled over things for a moment, then slipped into the room. He stuck his fingers into a crack in the stone wall. There was moss inside, but it would do for a handhold. He began to pull himself up one bit at a time.

Once he was high enough, he began looking for footholds, then he felt for the next place to put his hands and started climbing again. He wasn't exactly nimble, but compared to the tree he had climbed as a boy, this was easy.

Was that tree still there? Or was it gone now?

"Errggyahh… St…op…"

"GROBG! GRROROGB!!"

He ignored the sudden flash of memory, focusing his attention on the goblins. Fortunately (as fortunate as anything could be in this place), they didn't seem to have noticed him yet. His enemies' revelry didn't mean he was free to make noise, but a small amount of sound could go unnoticed.

The adventurer stopped where he was and steadied his breathing, then climbed just a little higher.

He checked his distance, then kicked off the wall as hard as he could.

He had no superhuman jumping capability. In his armor and helmet, all he could really do was drop like a stone.

But he only needed enough speed to crush a goblin underfoot. This would do nicely.

"GBOROB?!" One goblin shouted when something suddenly landed on him. The adventurer ignored him except to step on his neck. Two.

"GGB?! GOBOGORB!!"

"GRBG!!"

The ambushed goblins now yammered and got to their feet, but of course, he had been expecting that. He didn't waste a moment: he already had a dagger in each hand.

"GROOGBG?!"

"GORRG?!"

One goblin found a tossed knife protruding from his windpipe; he flailed his arms like he was drowning and then collapsed. Three.

Rather than bothering to watch the monster die, the adventurer pulled the spear from his belt in a reverse grip and thrust it behind him.

"GOBOOOGOB?!"

The goblin, slow to react because he had been so engrossed in jabbing the woman, thrashed as he was stabbed through the back. Four.

The captive shrieked as a geyser of blood came down on her head, but that didn't matter right now.

"GOOOROGOB!!"

The companions of the dead goblins were waving clubs that appeared to be made of wood. Taking the leader in an ambush was always best, but there were no guarantees. If he'd failed, it would have been a five-on-one fight, and he had wanted to avoid that.

He had chosen to even the odds a little first. Then the fight could really start.

"GOROBG! GGBGOROGB!!"

"Hrrr—ah!"

The club slammed down on what looked like the remains of a meal, scattering bits of it everywhere.

He jumped back to dodge it, drawing his strange-length sword with his right hand.

"Are you all right?"

"Ahh… Ugh…"

Immediately to his side was the woman the goblins had been torturing until a moment before. He spoke to her, but the response was faint and slow.

It would be difficult to do this without involving her. He couldn't retreat. The hobgoblin was closing in. The adventurer clicked his tongue.

"Hmph."

"GOROG?!" The great monster tried to continue his attack, but then cried out. It was because the adventurer had flung the red-hot pole rolling on the ground nearby with his foot.

The creature shouted and flailed, entirely missing the parallel between the current predicament and what they had been doing to the young woman a few minutes before.

The armored man, not about to miss such a ripe chance, raised his round shield and charged into his enemy.

"GROGORO!!"

"Hrrgh…!"

The club came at him again; he did his best to catch the attack early in the swing and divert it. He felt his left hand tingle from the impact.

But it was no longer a problem. He felt the sword in his right hand sink into the hobgoblin's gut, then he twisted it.

"GOROGOBOGOBOGOROBG?!" With a great howl, the hobgoblin dropped his club.

This would make five…

"GGBGRO!!"

"Hagh…?!"

But the next instant, he felt a massive fist connect with his head, and he went tumbling through the air. He landed in a corner of the hall, falling among the bones and scraps—no, rolling.

He had to if he wanted to avoid the fist that came crashing down the very next second.

The girls screamed—they had become numb to their surroundings but still retained instinctive fear—while he got to his feet, shaking his head.

It didn't die immediately?

He hadn't struck the hobgoblin in a vital place. Wait—he had more important things to do now.

He felt around near his feet, fighting against his wobbly, unsteady vision until he found something.

"GBOORGB?!"

A scream. The sound of shattering bones. He didn't know where he had hit it, but he'd hit it nonetheless.

"Ah... Hrah!"

"GOROGB?! GBRRG?! GOBOG?! GBBGB?!"

He closed the distance, raised his weapon, brought it down. Again. Once more. And then again.

Soon the hobgoblin's screams ceased, and the room was filled only with a watery smacking sound.

He finally let out a breath and looked at the implement in his hand.

It emitted a faint smoke; this was the shard of timber the goblins had been using to keep a fire going.

"...I see." He tossed it behind himself again, then braced a foot against the hobgoblin's stomach and pulled out his sword. It was followed by a pile of entrails, but he jabbed and slashed the creature again, just to be sure.

Stabbing it in the stomach hadn't killed it. Even a monster with a caved-in face could potentially stand again.

Finally, he wiped the blood off on a goblin's loincloth, returned the sword to his scabbard, and murmured, "Five... It wasn't supposed to be a small brood, though."

Most likely, the adventurers who had come to explore this place had thinned out the goblins' numbers. It was also likely that's how they got wiped out.

He considered that fact, accepted it, then shook his head.

It wouldn't do for him to misunderstand. It was a common story, but not inevitable, not even frequent. It was simply that there were always unlucky people, at all times and in all places. Maybe they were novices who lacked the knowledge or experience, or maybe they had tripped up in the middle of battle...

That was all it was, and nothing more.

All the more reason he shouldn't imagine that he was better than anyone else merely because he'd survived. His master had taught him that more than once, and here again he found himself keenly aware of the truth of that lesson.

After all, it was goblins who unequivocally believed they were always the best and most important things in the world.

He reminded himself of these things as he gathered the young women, the hapless survivors, picking them up and setting them down like so much luggage. He found the most presentable blankets from his own bags as well as from among the goblins' looted goods and used them to cover the women.

He did so in part because he didn't know their physical state, and partially because they must be exhausted.

All any of them could do was weep; when he saw that none of them was in a fit state to talk, he calmly gave them just the facts. "You'll be able to go home soon," he said, and then after a moment's thought, he added, "Just wait a little while."

No other comfort I might offer would have any meaning.

Now ignoring the wailing women behind him, he began rifling through the goblins' instruments of battle with a nonchalant hand. It hadn't been very long since the initial kidnapping this time, but he had seen goblin children before.

They might be hiding. He had learned that goblins were quick to reproduce.

Plus, he wanted to at least bring back the rank tags of the dead adventurers.

"......?"

In the muck, his hand brushed against something hard. He pulled it out and found a small ring set with a gemstone.

A ring of Mapping, perhaps?

No, it's not that.

He wiped off the grime and looked at the shimmering stone. He had never seen anything quite like it before, not that he was especially familiar with such things.

The inside almost seemed to be aflame, burning and burning without end.

"Hmm."

He tossed it nonchalantly into his bag and out of his mind.

He had other things to think about.

The goblin corpses. The kidnapped women. Getting everyone home safely and making his report.

After that, there was collecting his reward, preparing his equipment, finding the next quest, and killing goblins.

He wore grimy leather armor and a steel helmet with a broken horn on it. He carried a sword of a strange length at his hip and a small round shield on his arm.

For Goblin Slayer, as for the goblins, this was an ordinary day, just as terrible and ugly as all the others.

§

"Ahh, what fantastic weather!"

The sun and blue sky hanging overhead, Cow Girl flung white sheets over the clothesline. They gave an audible snap as they fluttered open.

She put the laundry in a washbasin with some ash, trod it clean, let it dry, and then gathered it together. The process took time and effort, but to her own surprise, once she got started, she enjoyed it, so much that she started openly chuckling to herself.

As for *him*, he had gotten to the point where he actually slept in the main house instead of in the shed. That meant more laundry—but maybe that was part of why she enjoyed it.

"♪"

Cow Girl hummed a little tune as she grabbed the next item: a shirt—*his* shirt. She had quietly gone into the shed and collected it while he was out. It was caked with dust, dirt, sweat, and what she thought was probably blood.

She could hardly just leave it that way. She was taken aback to see how thickly the water ran with grime as she worked the shirt with her feet. But then she gave it a firm flap to get the wrinkles out and nodded at it in satisfaction.

"Mm, excellent!"

There were still a few defiant stains, but the worst of the stuff had come off. That would do nicely. He did talk to *her*, a girl, almost every day. Surely it wasn't wrong to expect him to pay just the slightest bit of attention to his appearance.

"Then there's that armor of his…"

She put her chin in her hand and had a hard think. It was definitely dirty—at least, that was what she figured—but somehow it didn't seem likely he would clean it for her. And something in her hesitated to take it upon herself to shine the thing up. It was part of his work, his job, and that wasn't something she should intrude on.

His work…

Cow Girl briefly paused in her own labors and looked up at the sky. Adventure. Adventurers.

She felt so close to those words, and yet so far away.

He ensconced himself in his armor and helmet and delved caves or old ruins where he did battle with monsters.

The way she remembered him was from five years before, on the day of their fight… And then that boy she remembered reappeared before her as an adventurer.

On one level, she understood that one of those boys had become the other.

Yet on another, she couldn't for the life of her imagine that they were the same person.

"…This is a tough one." She ran a hand over her bangs, so much lighter after her escapade with some scissors. Her field of vision seemed wider now, too; she felt as if she could see things a little differently now, and yet, she still couldn't quite accept it all.

"Well, I guess it's not really anything to worry about… I think?"

Hmm? Cow Girl cocked her head in surprise. She had reached for the next piece of laundry, but her hand only grabbed empty air. When she looked over, she found there was nothing left in the washbasin.

Hmm. So she had cleaned it all up without even realizing it.

What to do?

She put her hand to her face instead, shading her eyes as she stared up at the sun. It was still high in the sky, too early to be done with work. There were the cows and pigs and chickens to attend to, of course, but they didn't need constant care. And though she tried to help out around the farm any way she could, her uncle rarely let her do anything too physical. She understood that he was concerned for her, knowing how she had been until very recently, but it still left her a bit dejected.

"Hmm...... Oh, got it!" She snapped her fingers awkwardly. She would make dinner. That would be good.

Nothing special motivated her; it was just an innocent, passing thought. To Cow Girl, though, it seemed like an excellent idea, and she started skipping toward the house—

"Whoops, hold on, hold on."

She grabbed the washbasin she had nearly forgotten, pouring out the water so the tub could dry. Then she jogged back to the house.

What to make? What did they even have? What could she cook well? She was familiar with her uncle's favorites, but...

"I wonder if *he'll* like them...?" she murmured, running a finger along her lips.

The possibility made her very happy. She pumped her arm, excited and ready to go.

§

"Sorry, can't buy it from ya."

"I see."

The stubborn old man dropped the ring on the counter, fixing the adventurer in front of him with a suspicious glare. "How'd y'come by the likes of this anyway?"

"I picked it up," Goblin Slayer replied. Then, almost as an afterthought, he added, "In some ruins. They had been turned into a goblin nest."

"Goblins, eh...?"

The equipment shop attached to the Guild was busy today, as it was almost every day. Goblin Slayer had boldly stridden in just after noon. From the grime and the smell that followed him, it was obvious he had come straight from an adventure.

"Urgh," griped an adventurer with a spear, seeming to have recognized Goblin Slayer, who ignored him.

"I need to restock," he announced.

So far, so typical—it was exactly how he had acted ever since becoming an adventurer. The craftsman was used to it by now.

Torch, herbs, salves, antidotes, wedges and other small items, knives and defensive equipment.

That's the shopping list of a ranger or a scout, not a warrior.

He had even come in once before requesting a bow and arrows. When the craftsman asked if he knew how to use them, the answer had been *"More or less."*

The old man had made a mental note that this visitor was as clever as he was eccentric.

What came next was different from usual.

Reaching into his item pouch to pay, the young man suddenly seemed to recall something and had produced the object in question.

The ring.

A circle of metal set with a gemstone that glittered as if on fire.

No—not *as if* on fire. Something inside the gem was actually burning.

"Will you buy it from me?"

He had set it on the countertop with such indifference. The shop-keeper had picked it up, fixing a jeweler's glass to one eye and taking a long, careful look. Finally, he shook his head.

"Sorry, can't buy it from ya."

Then came that look and the pointed question. The old man folded his arms and grunted thoughtfully, tapping his finger rhythmically on the counter.

"No question that ring's magical, but it's dangerous to handle before it's been identified."

"Can you identify it?"

"I can, but it's a pain."

The craftsman reached over and tapped a wooden sign hanging nearby. In several different writing systems it read WEAPONS & ARMOR BOUGHT AND SOLD. ITEMS IDENTIFIED—HALF PURCHASE PRICE. The inscription was accompanied by a series of pictures for the benefit of the illiterate. When dealing with adventurers, it was important to be accessible and, ideally, unflappable.

"Now, some people think that's highway robbery, but a man deserves to be compensated for his skills. No discounts."

"I see." Goblin Slayer looked pitiful even to the craftsman, the person who had made his gear. The adventurer seemed to be well enough aware that some derided him as filthy and strange.

An enchanted ring would demand a certain price. Would a still-green dungeon-diver like him be able to pay it…?

"D'you have the money?"

"I do," he replied, evoking an impressed "Ho" from the craftsman.

"Been saving up, have you?"

"Yes. I've been putting away the rewards from goblin hunting."

The old man nodded. Come to think of it, he'd heard this adventurer took quests relentlessly.

"But," Goblin Slayer added soberly, "I have plans for it. If the price is too high, I can't pay."

Them's the breaks, eh?

"S'pose you could always try just putting it on."

"I was sternly warned never to put on a strange ring."

"And a wise warning it was." Then the craftsman let out a long, deep breath, as though he had only just now thought of something. "…Hrm, that's right."

What of it? He was old enough now. He could show a little kindness toward some young pup once in a while if he wanted.

"There might be some other adventurer who can identify it. Maybe ask around, eh?"

"…Other adventurers," Goblin Slayer murmured shortly, then he swept up the ring, flung it back in his bag, and nodded. "Understood."

"I wonder if you do," the old man said from behind him as he strode out of the room.

It was a fair question—and indeed, there was something about this the young man hadn't yet grasped.

Oh, he understood well enough that the ring had to be identified before he could sell it, and that he could ask another adventurer to evaluate the thing for him. The problem was…

"Hmm."

Goblin Slayer entered the Guild waiting area, taking in all the adventurers around him. But every single one of them seemed to act as if he weren't there.

They weren't exactly avoiding him, per se. But neither was he getting any encouraging looks. Instead, many a suspicious glance was directed at this young man notorious for his eccentric habit of hunting nothing but goblins.

In a word, he received no more interest than any other grimy novice.

That was all they took him for. And that was the problem.

"Identification."

Who here would be able to help him with that task? He didn't have the slightest idea what sorts of jobs the other adventurers even did.

Goblin Slayer grunted softly and went to sit on a bench in a corner of the waiting area.

It was the bench farthest from the door. If what you wanted was first pick of the quests, it was the worst possible place to be, but he knew he didn't have to hurry; the goblin quests would still be there. He thought it would be good to sit down here, where he would be out of the way of the other adventurers.

With a quick motion, Goblin Slayer pulled the ring back out of his bag and held it up to the window light. He could just see the other adventurers going about their business at the Guild through the flickering flame at the ring's center.

To the right, to the left. Looking at the board, laughing with their friends, going to the front desk or setting out on a journey.

He watched it all aimlessly. Many different adventurers, doing many different things.

And why?

When he thought about it, he couldn't see any real meaning in it.

If something was useful, he would use it. If he could sell it, the money would go into his war chest. And if it was neither useful nor valuable, he would throw it away.

That was what he should do. Nothing to regret.

"Um, excuse me…"

It was just at that moment that a rather hesitant voice spoke to him.

"…Is something the matter, sir?"

In front of him, he saw a female staff member of the Guild, her hair tied gently in a braid. He didn't have to search his memory to know who she was. She had helped him out any number of times.

It was Guild Girl.

"It is nothing important," he said and showed her the ring in his hand.

The glittering flame inside its gemstone provoked a gasp of amazement from Guild Girl. "What a lovely ring. Did you find it in some ruins or something?"

"No." Goblin Slayer shook his head. "I found it in a goblin nest."

"Really..." Guild Girl didn't look quite sure what to say next. He glanced questioningly at her, and she shook her head, causing her braid to bounce, then smiled. "I guess you are *Goblin* Slayer."

"Yes." He nodded. "I've been looking for someone to identify this ring."

"You..." Guild Girl blinked. "...*were?*"

"I don't know who to ask." He tossed the ring casually back in his bag, letting out a soft sigh as he did so. "So just now, I decided to simply throw it away.

"There's no point in carrying around something you can't use," he murmured, and Guild Girl's expression grew more ambiguous still.

"What?" Goblin Slayer grunted, unable to read what she was thinking.

"Oh, uh..." Her shoulders jumped in surprise, and she fiddled uncertainly with her hair. "I, er... I might be able to introduce you to someone."

§

"...Well, now?"

The witch had come into the Guild just as usual, but now she blinked and arched one of her long eyebrows. Guild Girl was waving at her to come over. And what was more, beside her was—

"..."

Witch's lips relaxed into a small smile, and she headed over, hips swaying. Adventurers around the room stole glances at her voluptuous body and whispered to one another. But she pulled her wide-brimmed hat down over her eyes and returned none of their looks.

What worth could there be in the words of people who didn't even have the nerve to talk to her face-to-face? She almost seemed to be enjoying the room's reaction as she made her way along, shaking her head gently.

"And, what…could this be about?" Her breathy voice seemed to catch ever so slightly. Her generous chest shifted each time she drew a breath. She chuckled, a sound she made deep in her throat, then spoke the name of the man before her like a mischievous child. "Goblin, Slayer?"

"I have a request." The man in the grimy leather armor and cheap-looking steel helmet could not have been more blunt or disinterested. "Are you able to perform identifications?"

"Identifications…?" Witch couldn't seem to decide what he wanted—or perhaps she understood exactly what he was asking, and that was what prompted her questioning look.

Watching over the exchange from the side, Guild Girl gave an uncomfortable laugh and, hoping to rescue the situation, said, "Uh, you see… Our friend Goblin Slayer, he found a ring in some ruins."

"Ah, haa…" Witch narrowed her eyes deliberately before nodding. "That…explains it."

"Right. He wants to know if you could have a look at it…"

Witch reached out a slim, pale arm, beckoning to the man. "May I, see it?"

"Here." Goblin Slayer nonchalantly went through his bag and produced the ring.

"Well, now…" Witch made an admiring sound. Even Guild Girl, seeing the ring for the second time, widened her eyes and breathed, "Wow…"

The metal circle glinted faintly. Guild Girl hadn't realized earlier just how modest it was. It didn't *look* like an item that contained a powerful magic; it didn't even look like it would command much value as a piece of jewelry. But the shimmering inside that gemstone somehow captured the heart.

Witch took the ring in her hand and gazed at it in the sunlight coming through the window. She caressed it as if feeling it out with her fingertips, turned it over to see if there was any writing engraved on the inside.

A moment later, she shook her head gently. "I'm...sorry." She offered the ring back along with her words. Goblin Slayer took it and put it back in his bag. "I'm, not...quite sure...what it is."

"I see." There was no hint of disappointment in his response. He just said calmly, "Sorry to bother you."

If anything, Guild Girl was more disappointed than he was; she murmured, "Is that right? What a shame."

"No," he said with a shake of his head. "It simply means I will get rid of it."

Witch, however, was not done talking. "But...listen." She practically draped herself over her own staff, pointing a finger to indicate his item bag. "That thing... I know, someone...who, might want exactly...what you, have there."

"Hmm." Goblin Slayer grunted and reached into the bag once more. "I will give it to you, then."

"...Heh, heh... There's, no greed...in you, is there?"

Hmm, hmm. There was that quiet chuckle again. Then Witch told him where to find the person in question, as melodically as if she were intoning a spell. It was nothing so distinguished as an actual address, but rather a vague description of a spot beside a river outside town.

"Just...go there. I should think...she'll be there...at, any time."

"I see." Goblin Slayer nodded. "That helps."

"Don't, mention it," Witch said with another slow shake of her head. "I was, glad to see...what you showed me." Then she seemed to remember something and added, "Apple cider... Perhaps you ought, to bring some...along?"

Goblin Slayer thought this over for a moment then, with a tilt of his helmet, replied softly, "Understood. Thanks. You've been helpful."

And then he strode boldly away.

For a second, Guild Girl seemed surprised to have been so summarily left behind, but she soon murmured, "Oh," and smiled. It had taken her a moment, but she had figured out whom those last few words were directed at.

"Not at all!" she called to his swiftly receding back, waving her hand. Even though she knew she wouldn't get a response.

"So...?" Witch smiled at Guild Girl like a cat toying with a mouse.

"Y-yes?" Guild Girl asked. Her shoulders trembled, causing Witch's smile to deepen.

"Perhaps...you could, give me...something, as a reward?"

"Wh-who, me?"

Uh-oh. Guild Girl frowned now, concerned. Did she want money? Guild Girl was still paid the starting salary and didn't have much to spare.

"Say... Do you, perchance...know any, adventurers...who can handle, a spear...?"

"Huh?" Guild Girl, roused from her troubled ruminations, blinked. After a moment's thought, she said, "Oh yes." Yes, she did know someone like that. A sharp new adventurer. In fact, she had worked with him herself.

"The one who, fought that...centipede. He often...asks me, to work with him...temporarily. But..."

She got along fairly well with him. They could banter with each other. It might have been fair to call them friends.

But, she said. Witch's voice was small and hesitant, only just above a whisper.

She wanted to form a proper party with him...

Guild Girl giggled; Witch looked so young and innocent making this shy request.

"But of course. Just leave it to me!"

§

He'd been told he would know it when he saw it, and indeed he did.

For a while he had been walking down well-traveled streets, the jug of apple cider he'd bought at the tavern hanging from one hand.

Where he would normally head toward the farm for the night, though, he went in exactly the opposite direction, until he reached the outskirts of town. There he found what perhaps would be best described as a hovel.

A waterwheel creaked in the river nearby, and smoke drifted from the chimney of the small building. It was sturdier than a simple hut but too modest to be called a proper house.

Which makes it a hovel, after all.

By the time he had reached this conclusion, Goblin Slayer was standing in front of the weathered door. Only the knocker shone brightly, as if it alone were new; it looked out of place on this building.

I will have to do a more careful study of the geography around here.

He felt a pang as he realized how little he knew about what was in the area around town. He should have pounded the details into his head. But he hadn't known about this hovel until this very moment.

Swallowing his frustration with himself, he gave a few firm strikes with the knocker.

"Pardon me," he called to whoever was inside. "I have something I would like to have identified."

There was no response.

He stood in front of the door for several seconds longer.

Still no answer. Goblin Slayer, continuing to stand there, grunted softly. He was certain the occupant was home. If Witch hadn't implied as much, the smoke from the chimney would still have been a giveaway.

To receive no answer from someone who wasn't home was one thing; but if she wasn't going to answer even when she was home, then there would be no point in coming back another time.

He knocked again, harder this time.

"Pardon me. I have something I would like to have identified."

This time, a voice came from within: "Oh, it's open. Just come on in."

There was a note of impudence in the invitation, but Goblin Slayer paid it no mind as he opened the door. The haughtiness wasn't so different from the way he acted. He figured he should be grateful she had replied at all.

Inside the little house—well, the first thing he had to decide was where to walk. The place was, in a word, buried. Piles of old books and children's toys—or were they just junk?—were scattered around. Visible plates were loaded with table scraps.

A pair of bellows worked over by the hearth with a metallic screech; a rope was strung across the ceiling, and laundry had been hung from it.

As far back in that room as one could get, in the slightest of open spaces, a shadow leaned over a desk, squirming. When he got close enough—moving slowly, carefully, so as not to bump into anything—he finally realized the shape was a person.

It was someone who looked like a wizard, in fact, although the robes were covered in patches from top to bottom. There was something on the desk in front of them. "*No, not like that,*" the wizard was muttering. "*No, not that, either.*"

Cards.

Cards with colors and pictures of all sorts on them—the wizard would pile them up only to slide them apart again, then shuffle and cut the deck.

The figure hardly seemed to notice Goblin Slayer standing behind them. He watched them for a moment, and then, when they didn't say anything, he quietly offered, "I would like to request the identification of a ring."

"Hmmm…? Oh, a ring. Oh yeah? That so? A ring…"

The voice was younger, higher-pitched than he'd expected, but regardless, didn't sound very interested. The wizard continued to move the cards around, chin in hand, muttering something.

"A ring?!"

Suddenly, the mage jumped up with a clatter, and the cards went flying as if a blizzard had blown them away. At the same time, the hood covering the wizard's head fell away with a flutter.

Dull gold hair, clipped more or less to the shoulders, tumbled out.

"Don't tell me! You've not found Spark, have you?!" The wizard who clutched at his leather breastplate was female.

So it was a woman?

Behind his visor, Goblin Slayer blinked.

The wizard's hair was wild, sticking out this way and that—maybe she never combed it, or maybe trying wouldn't do any good.

She quickly ran a hand through the hair, producing a whiff of a not-unpleasant aroma.

From this distance, he could see her eyes, which seemed to be green. But they were distorted by her spectacles, and the color was strangely indistinct.

An outer garment made from the fur of an animal he couldn't identify reached down to the woman's knees. He had no idea whether it was intended to be that short, or if the wizard just didn't care whether or not it fit. When she covered the entire thing with an outer robe, voilà—it was enough to conceal her gender.

"No, but wait, we mustn't jump to conclusions!" the wizard rebuked herself. "First, let me see the ring!" And then she drew back again, leaving Goblin Slayer in place, flummoxed.

"..." He didn't know exactly what to say, but he had come here precisely to show her the ring. Goblin Slayer offered the item in question; and indeed, the ring shimmered faintly in the dim room. Although it was noontime, the house was dim because the books were piled so high that they blocked the windows. There was just enough light to make the drifting dust inside visible; the motes floated about, twinkling like fireflies.

"This is it."

"Ha-ha...! Is it, now? Let me... Here, let me look."

The wizard dispensed with pleasantries, urging him along like an impatient child. Then she grabbed the ring.

She opened her eyes wide as she leaned toward the gleaming object, studying it as closely as she could. She didn't seem to quite comprehend what the light was, but she looked like a kid seeing her first rainbow.

At last, her lips moved as if she was giving a kiss; she murmured a word, then two.

When she did so, the ring in her white palm began to project a faint halo, and then the gleaming seemed to increase. Little flecks of light flew from it like tiny fireworks, jumping and then fading like shooting stars.

They were sparks, indeed.

A moment later, they stilled again, sinking back into the gem at the center of the ring.

The woman watched all this, then rubbed her eyes, nodding and making pleased noises.

"…Where'd you get this?"

"A goblin nest."

"Goblins had it? *Goblins?!*"

"That's correct." Goblin Slayer nodded. "It was with the trash near their sleeping chamber."

"Ha… Ha-ha! Ha-ha-ha-ha-ha-ha-ha-ha-ha-ha!!"

In an instant, all seriousness vanished from her expression; she slapped her knee, laughing uproariously, practically rolling on the floor. She hugged her stomach, then finally began pounding her desk in hilarity.

"Ohhhh, ha-ha-ha! Did they—did they really? Now *that's* something I wouldn't have imagined!"

"…"

"And here everyone thinks a magic ring you find in a cave is the least, most disreputable thing!"

True. Goblin Slayer nodded. He recalled his master saying something similar.

"Oops," the woman said, reaching out to a pile of junk on the desk that threatened to fall over from the shock of her slapping and shouting.

Goblin Slayer waited, but the answer he wanted never came, so he asked the question himself.

"Tell me, what is the effect of that ring?"

"Not much, for most people," the wizard replied. She settled luxuriously into her chair, pointedly crossing and recrossing her legs. Her muscles were taut and toned, despite the fact that she didn't seem to get out much. "But personally, I find it very valuable."

"And what about me?"

"Dunno. It's a Breath ring, see? It lets you breathe anywhere. Literally anywhere."

"Hmm."

"Whatcha think?" The corners of her lips rose in a smile like a spider weaving a web. "Think you'd be interested in selling it to me?"

She leaned in so close, she seemed about to plant a kiss on Goblin Slayer's helmet. "I'll pay anything. In fact—" There was that smile again. "I'll *do* anything, for this."

An unusual scent drifted through the air. It wasn't alcohol. Maybe herbs, he guessed.

Goblin Slayer grunted softly. "You are willing to give something other than money, then."

"Bet on it."

"I see."

She nodded at him, ready for what he would ask. Goblin Slayer spoke without hesitation.

"I want something that will help me kill goblins."

"……Huh?" The wizard blinked, and then, apparently unable to contain herself, burst out laughing again. "Hhh—ggh… Hkhk… B-bwa! G-goblins?! Goblins, he says!"

Under the assault of all this protracted shouting, the stuff on the desk finally collapsed.

The wizard practically fell out of her chair, her body twisting with laughter, her eyes running with tears.

"Hah—he-he… Hoo, hkhkhk… What a— *What a…*!"

Her ample chest bounced as she gasped for air.

Goblin Slayer waited until she calmed down, then added as if he had just remembered, "I will also offer you apple cider."

"Spa…spa…s-spare meee…!"

She smacked the desk a couple more times, at which the deck of cards proceeded to scatter everywhere.

And so Goblin Slayer was confronted by a woman contorting with laughter on the floor, surrounded by a great cloud of dust.

Such was his meeting with the magus of electricity, Arc Mage.

"Eeeeeeeeeeek!!"

A woman's high-pitched scream echoed throughout the abandoned mine, accompanied by a fleshy smacking and a muffled yell.

The girl's upraised foot had struck the goblin square in the jaw. The little devil thumped to the ground, frothing blood: a critical hit, no question.

Well, that was goblins for you. There was no need for any special weapons or skills to kill them.

"Why would goblins set up in an abandoned mine anyway?" The martial artist girl asked, not even bothering to set down her leg.

The young warrior frowned. "...I heard there was a battle to the east. Maybe they came from there."

"Huh? Through the central region? Sounds like a lot of trouble to me."

"Traveling underground, you can go anywhere," the young warrior said, trying to forestall unpleasant memories. He took his hand off his sword, which he hadn't even needed to draw.

"*Makes sense,*" the girl added, impressed. He didn't want to just foist much of the fighting on her, but there wasn't much choice. It was hard to keep an eye on everyone from the very front of the formation. But if he were second or third in line, his weapon couldn't reach the enemy.

Maybe I should take up the spear like a certain someone I know...

As he considered the possibility, Young Warrior turned to the man behind him. "What do you think, Professor?"

"Hrm, lessee," the man they called Professor replied in a surprisingly brusque voice. If one lifted up his weathered coat, a wolflike face would have been visible. He was a padfoot wizard, approaching middle age—suggesting that he had given up life as a lecturer to pursue a dream of adventuring. Fangs bared, he continued, "All this dust gets in my nose, keeps it from working right. And all these crisscrossing paths make mapping a tall order."

"We only need the rough outline. We're not here for an official survey or anything."

Right, right. The padfoot wizard nodded amiably and began sketching on his sheepskin paper.

I made the right choice, having him be our cartographer, Young Warrior thought, impressed by the man's calm demeanor. His skill was necessary to collect their reward from this quest, and besides, the ability to keep a cool head was always valuable. He inspired far more confidence than some hot-tempered spell caster who seemed liable to fire off magic at the slightest provocation. But then there was—

"—? Is something the matter?" The young woman looked at him in confusion, her long hair hanging down. But even she was all right. The problem was the other two.

"Heeey, looks like it just keeps goin' this way!"

"You have no idea how hard I worked to keep this young lady from getting too far ahead."

From the darkness emerged a dwarf girl, so young she still hadn't grown her beard, and an elf boy.

Well, it wasn't actually that easy to tell how old they really were. The dwarf fancied herself as a scout-in-training; the elf was someone who had discovered his faith in the Earth Mother. That was all the young warrior knew about them, and for the time being, it was all he needed to know.

"Whazzat?! We hardly made any progress before you were all, *Let's go back, let's turn around, ooh, I'm so scared!*"

"Be serious. I'll have you know we simply see things differently from dwarves."

Young Warrior had sent them on ahead because both of them could see in the dark, but the reconnaissance mission had quickly degenerated into this. He put a hand to his face.

Glad they get along so well...

He thought of his former—he was loath to say *departed*—companions. He realized now how hard that monk had worked to lead them. He would have to apologize someday.

"It's great you're such good friends," Martial Artist said with a broad smile. It didn't seem he could expect any intervention from the flummoxed-looking padfoot wizard, either.

"Excuse me," the warrior said, maintaining his calm, "but I asked you to scout ahead, not get into an argument."

"Hmph!" The dwarf girl puffed out her cheeks, while the elf priest gave her a triumphant smirk.

"And I asked *you* to go with her, not to let her bait you into a fight."

"...Hrmm." Elf Acolyte tried to keep the smile on his face, but the dwarf girl now glared at him.

"Look, you even got me yelled at," she said.

"Who got who yelled at? You started it."

"Says the guy who lost everything gambling, got alms from a nun, and suddenly found religion."

"Hrgh?!"

This was something of a critical hit in its own way.

The dwarf, brought up in the military, knew how to handle herself in an argument, and if she lacked something in intellect vis-à-vis the elf, she certainly had him beat on experience.

The elf fell silent as the dwarf cackled beside him; the warrior decided that was enough for now and got ready to move on.

"Okay, form up and let's go deeper. We'll have to report the appearance of goblins eventually, but..."

"The map's not finished yet, huh?" the silver-haired fighter asked.

"Right," the warrior replied, and then he took a step farther into the mine. Whereupon...

"...Well, this won't do at all. What a terrible smell," Professor grunted suddenly.

Young Warrior instantly had his sword in his hand. "You, the Odd

Couple, look after the Professor. Me and the girl will be out in front. Professor, get ready with your magic."

"Wha? Wha?"

"Hey, who's an odd couple…?!"

Martial Artist was thoroughly confused, and the elf was incensed, but Young Warrior ignored them both, fixing his eyes on the darkness ahead, straining his ears to hear.

The first thing he detected was innumerable footsteps. Then came the awful stench. And finally, the eyes glowing faintly in the darkness.

What to do about helmets?

There were a lot of enemies. In a pitched battle, wouldn't it be a bad thing if the commander couldn't survey the whole field?

After an instant's consideration of the helmet hanging on his back, he tossed the equipment away, though for a different reason from before.

"Shoulda bought a bowl helmet…"

"Goblins, and…something very big!"

The greenskins poured out of the darkness.

"GOORRBGG…"

"GOROB! GGBBRROG!"

Four, no, five of them. They had crude weapons in their hands. That was good. Not *good*, but good.

"GBRRRRR!"

And then there was the creature leading this little band, a giant who towered almost to the ceiling of the mine tunnel. With the club it swung thoughtlessly in its hand, it was a profoundly intimidating sight.

Young Warrior recognized it. He had never seen one, but he'd heard tell of them in his last party, albeit briefly.

"A hob!"

"Well, strictly speaking, that means *giant* in the old tongue," the padfoot wizard said nonchalantly. Maybe the warrior shouldn't have been surprised that he was already forming sigils with his hands.

"It has the whiff of poison," Elf Acolyte said importantly. "I suppose it will be my job to neutralize that."

"Seeing as that's the only miracle you've got, yeah, I guess so," the dwarf quipped.

"Hmph. This is not the time for talk."

"If you say so." The dwarf girl pulled out something that looked like a cross between a billhook and dagger and held it in reverse grip. She knew it would be her responsibility to protect their spell casters. Young Warrior nodded.

"My armor's the thickest," he said, "so I'll handle the goblins. Their poisoned blades will be less likely to get through my armor. And you—"

"Take the big one! Got it!" Martial Artist called out excitedly. As she sprang forward at the enemy, the battle began.

"GRRORB!"

"GBR!!"

These were goblins they were dealing with. Young Warrior cast a glance to either side, mindful of the possibility the enemy might break through the walls (an unpleasant memory), then he advanced.

Trying to swing a two-handed sword like a madman would gain him nothing in this confined space, but...

"Hrr—aagghh!"

He made a sidelong sweep with his blade. The tunnel just barely accommodated the move, the tip scraping along the wall.

"GOOBR?!"

At that same instant, a glistening dagger bounced off his sword. A goblin flinched back.

So it was *poisoned, huh?*

But everything was well in hand. The warrior licked his lips, dry with the anxiety of combat, and brought his sword back to center.

Provoke, parry, and when he was close enough, launch an attack of opportunity.

His role was to be the tank. The heart of their assault would be the young woman currently rushing through the enemy ranks, shooting through the heart of the foe like an arrow.

"GGGBBORG!!"

Naturally, no monster would be very disturbed by the sight of one unarmed girl charging at them.

This monster took a snorting breath, raising a club until it brushed the ceiling of the narrow cave, then brought it down with deadly force.

"Yah!" Martial Artist twisted away from the arc of the weapon. Her hair spun and floated from the resulting air pressure. "Hiii-yah!"

Then she dropped her hips into a deep stance and thrust her fist out in front of her. There was a ringing, like that of a great bell.

"GOOB?!"

Ripples spread across the hobgoblin's hideously distended belly, and the giant stumbled a step back.

But that was all. The massive goblin looked down at his stomach in confusion, then produced an awful grin.

"GGGGGG…!"

"Yikes, what's going on here? That thing is *soft!*"

The thick layers of fat acted like a kind of armor themselves, protecting the creature from any real harm. As the girl learned to her chagrin.

"Don't get distracted—keep at it!"

"GOOROGB?!"

The warrior had diverted a goblin's attack to the side, his sword at a slant, then retaliated immediately with a cut, landing his first kill. He was already kicking the corpse away as he shouted to Martial Artist, who replied, "Okay!"

"Ahh… Hup!" A dart came flying from behind Young Warrior, taking advantage of the attack of opportunity he'd created.

"GBRO?!" A goblin exclaimed when the dart buried itself in his hand, earning Young Warrior enough time to reform his stance.

"Heh-heh-heh! These trick bows are rather fun," Elf Acolyte said. He was holding a spring-loaded dart gun.

The dwarf girl, standing beside him with her dagger in hand, grumbled, "What happened to the precepts of the Earth Mother?"

"Don't insult me. This is a minimalist weapon, strictly for self-defense."

That explained why the elf didn't have any money. The warrior smirked, then slashed another goblin.

"GOOBORG?!"

That made two. Reloading that little toy of the elf's would take time. He didn't want to count on it for anything.

It was Dwarf Scout's presence and protection that allowed Elf

Acolyte the luxury of simply standing and shooting. In fact, she had to protect all three of the people on their back row. Young Warrior believed he could trust her with this.

He focused forward and saw that the battle between Martial Artist and the hobgoblin was still going on.

"Hrr—hah!"

"GOOOG! GOROBG!!"

But exactly the sort of thing that often occurs in these fights happened to her.

Maybe she was overenthusiastic. Maybe she got her distancing wrong. In any event, the hobgoblin caught her leg and stopped her cold.

"Hrk?! Ahh?!"

"GOROGB! GOOOGBGR!!"

The hobgoblin's expression twisted hideously, while Martial Artist's face was seized with fear.

Would the creature crush her leg or simply swing her around helplessly? Goblins possessed a child's cruelty.

"Professor!"

"*Arma...Fugio...Amittimus!* Weapons, flee and be lost!"

Later, he would reflect that making the calm, restrained padfoot the last in line had been something of a stroke of genius. The old wizard was already conjuring up the right spell before Young Warrior had to ask for it.

Words of true power were released by this invocation and assailed the hobgoblin.

"?!"

"...!"

The first way the Fumble spell manifested was to pop the club right out of the goblin's hand.

Now Martial Artist's eyes shone. Her leg whipped around in the creature's grasp.

"HIIIIIII-YAH!" With a screech like a bird of prey, she pushed off her opponent's own hand to launch a flying kick. She came in, spinning like a top, smashing into the hobgoblin's face.

"GBORG?!" The scream could barely be heard over the crunch

of breaking bones. Blood gushed from the monster's broken nose, and it crumpled to the ground without another sound. The Professor later explained the most likely scenario was that a piece of bone had been driven into its brain.

Now that was a critical hit.

"Hup... Ah... Man, that was a close one...!" Martial Artist landed unsteadily on her feet, putting a relieved hand to her ample bust.

Young Warrior let out a deep breath, said, "Good," and again set upon the goblins in front of him.

"GOBORG?!"

"GRG?! GOOBG?!"

There were just three of them left, and their leader was dead.

We can do without a description of the rest; the party finished off the monsters, every last one.

Now, then.

With the fight over, what remained was to go through the goblins' possessions.

"Ahem, let's see here. It's not like I'm expecting goblins to have anything worthwhile on them, but..."

It was, of course, Dwarf Scout who reached out, grinning, toward the corpses. Young Warrior was staggered by how nimble her large fingers were. But he had other things to worry about.

He searched in the baggage for the water pouch. When he found it, he looked over at the padfoot wizard.

"Go ahead, both of you," the old beast replied. "I don't mind. Beauty before age!"

"Thanks."

The young man headed slightly down the tunnel to where the girl was sitting in a corner. As he drew near, she looked up at him with a cheerful but strained expression; she seemed hesitant.

"...Here." Instead of pointing any of this out, he sat down next to her and offered her the water.

"...Thanks, I'll have some."

The martial artist girl tried to take the skin, but her hands were trembling too badly. Was it nerves? Terror?

"Gosh, uh... Adventuring, it's... It's a lot..."

"A lot scarier than you thought, right?"

"...I thought I was going to die there," she whispered. Then she managed two swigs before closing the pouch.

"Yeah, it was bad." Young Warrior nodded, letting the waterskin she passed him roll around in his hands. "I was scared, too. But, well, I guess that's better than not being scared."

"...Is it?"

"If you weren't scared, I think you'd pretty much be on your way to dying."

Of course, sometimes you die even if you are scared.

The little addendum provoked a "What the heck?" from Martial Artist. Her smile was forced, but it was there.

"Scared of a bunch of goblins. There go my bragging rights, huh?" There was a note of disappointment, even disgust, in her voice. "And here I told Momma and Poppa that I was gonna go out into the world and make my fortune."

"You think being scared shitless by a Rock Eater's any better?"

"A rock what?" She tilted her head in perplexity, her silver hair cascading down. *Never mind*, he gestured with a half smile and a shake of his head.

It was so completely different. Different from *her*. Different from his last party.

"Anyway, not everything goes right the first time. Long as you're alive, you'll get another chance."

"...Right."

Because things had been so different, he wasn't sure if the words would be any real comfort to her. Maybe they were simply what he wished somebody had said to him.

The girl gave a nod, short but determined, and to his own surprise, that made him...happy.

"Hey, this hob's got a letter! Not that I can read it!"

"Ah, dwarves, as smart as you are tall. Give it here... Hmph, I thought so. So that's the story."

"If I can't read it, there's no way you can—is there?!"

Over by the hobgoblin, the elf and the dwarf were quarreling noisily. The old wizard, a pained smile on his face, worked his way between them. When he had retrieved the grimy sheet of paper, he nodded knowingly and said, "Ahh. These aren't letters so much as pictographs. Most likely they mean something akin to *Wait for orders.*"

"Pictographs... So goblins can't read?"

"Not necessarily. Judging by the style here, I would say it was a warlock who wrote this, perhaps..."

He didn't sound personally concerned about it. Considering the size of the mine, they had to be nearly through with their expedition.

Young Warrior, watching the whole scene distractedly, suddenly asked, "Hey, can you read and write?"

"Not a word!" the dwarf girl answered, puffing out her ample chest with something suspiciously like pride.

Young Warrior smiled. "Well, maybe you can learn when you get a chance. You and me both, together."

"Sure!"

Gotta keep going, a little longer.

That's what he would say to that bald-headed monk when the man got back to town. Maybe over drinks.

His choice made, Young Warrior got slowly to his feet.

CHAPTER 3

THE ELECTRIC MAGUS

"Mn… Ergh… Ooh?"

Cow Girl opened her eyes at what seemed to be a soft sound and the sensation of something moving.

Her body was stiff and hot; her throat burned, and her head hurt.

Did I fall asleep?

She was lying on the table, and when she sat up, she felt a blanket flutter to the floor. Her uncle must have put it on her.

The sky was already bright outside, but the air had a chill that tickled her skin.

Cow Girl rubbed her eyes, looking around a room illuminated by the pale light of dawn.

"—?!"

She jerked upright when she saw a shadow huddling in the corner. She let out a squeak, but she quickly relaxed again when she realized what it was.

"Oh, it's just you…"

"So you are awake." There was a clunk as he placed what seemed to be a leather pouch on the table.

The looming shape of the armored form, covered in gruesome stains, was just visible in the dimness. That was bad for the heart.

Cow Girl let out a relieved sigh, putting a hand to her chest to calm her racing pulse.

"Hey… How about you take that stuff off when you come home?" Her tone was confused, troubled.

"I can't let down my guard," he replied—softly, shortly. Cow Girl didn't really understand what he meant.

"Well, okay," she said, setting aside her confusion and starting to get to her feet. "How about I make some breakf—?"

"Don't need it," he said before she could finish. Cow Girl was speechless.

"I'll be out again soon," he continued. "Goblin hunting."

"Uh, but…"

Confused again, Cow Girl didn't quite know what to do with her eyes. They wandered around, taking in a kitchen that she knew very well. And in it, something resembling a person.

She swallowed. Her voice trembled the slightest bit as she asked, "But you…you just got home, didn't you…?"

"I was taking care of something else today." His voice was terribly quiet, nonchalant. She suspected that was how he talked to everyone, not just her. Somehow, it reminded her of the breeze blowing through a field on a dark night. "But now, I'm going to work."

Then he walked past her, barging through, and put his hand to the doorknob.

"But— Your room— I cleaned your room and washed the sheets…"

"I see."

That was all he said. Then he opened the door and closed it behind him, and then she was alone.

She hadn't even been able to tell him that maybe he ought to sleep, or at least eat.

Hargh. She sighed and slumped down in the chair again. She found herself flopping toward the ground.

"I just don't get it…"

She had decided to do her best. Decided not to mope or whine. So what should she do now?

Cow Girl had no idea what the answer to that question was. She leaned her forehead against the table, still warm with her own body heat.

There he goes again… Talk about single-minded!

He had work to do, so maybe it was inevitable, but she felt like he spent more time away from home than at it.

Could it be…like *that*?

But her thoughts were hazy, and no matter how she tried, nothing quite came together for her.

Until five years before, her father and mother had always been at home with her. And then after that, her uncle had always been here. But how would it be for a child whose parents had been tradespeople? She realized that such a person might not remember their names— maybe not even their faces.

"Agh…" Cow Girl sighed again, deep and long. Suddenly, she heard a creaking sound.

"Sighing so deep so early in the morning?"

"Uncle…" Cow Girl heaved herself upright and said "Good morning" in a voice that sounded pitiful even to her.

Her uncle, just woken up, stretched his stiff body and muttered in something that sounded like annoyance. "You'll catch cold, sleeping there."

"I know. You're right, but…"

She found she couldn't say *I was waiting for him*. Instead, she slowly got to her feet.

"Breakfast… I'll take care of it. It'll just be last night's soup, though."

"Much obliged."

Now it was her uncle who sat in a chair in the dining room, while Cow Girl shuffled off to the kitchen. She tossed on an apron and peered into the stove. The stove had gone completely cold, nothing but a pile of chill ashes and a small, lidded clay pot inside.

Cow Girl began by scraping the ashes together, carefully putting them into a jar, making sure none fell on the floor. Ash was precious, good for cleaning the stewpot or doing the laundry. It would be a waste to let any get away.

Once the inside of the stove was clean, she piled in some kindling and grasses to get the fire started. Then she pulled the pot out and used a pair of bellows to blow on yesterday's embers.

Happily, the fire caught, and the stove soon began burning.

"That'll do," Cow Girl said, clapping her hands gently to dust them off as she stood up.

"…Hmm?" Meanwhile, her uncle seemed to have noticed the leather pouch on the table.

Cow Girl peeked in from the other room. "Oh, he left that here, I think."

"Hrm, he's back?"

"And gone again."

Heh-heh, she chuckled shyly, or perhaps bitterly. Cow Girl went back to her work, feeling uncomfortable.

She thumped the stewpot down, then decided to skewer some bread and cook it.

"…Rent, eh?" There was a metallic jangling. Her uncle had opened the pouch and found money inside.

Cow Girl glanced into the other room again. Only bronze and silver coins filled the pouch, but there were quite a few of them.

"Wow," she breathed, causing her uncle to look in her direction and sigh.

"Awfully conscientious of him, considering he hardly even sleeps here."

"I guess maybe he's busy?" Cow Girl aimlessly—well, there was an aim, but still—stirred the pot. "Although, I have to admit…that isn't really how I pictured adventurers."

"Maybe so. I don't have a lot of experience with their kind, myself."

"Huh" was the only response Cow Girl gave to this.

Perhaps they would gain a bit of experience, then, as they went along. Then one day they might figure it out.

They might find out, for example, what an adventurer's life was like, how they could help. That sort of thing…

As Cow Girl knelt down to check the fire, she heard her uncle muse, "Or perhaps he has a lover somewhere."

"＿＿!"

For reasons even she couldn't begin to comprehend, Cow Girl felt a shock jolt through her body and jumped to her feet.

Her eyes met those of her startled uncle, who had glanced over. "A-are you all right…?"

©Shingo Adachi

"I'm f-fine, it's nothing…"

But then, but still, it couldn't be. Her head felt like a whirlpool, spinning round and round.

"A lover… Y-you don't really mean that…do you?"

What was going on? Why was her voice scratching like that?

"I suppose not," her uncle said. "You'd think a man in love would pay more attention to how he looked."

"Y-yeah, exactly!"

Cow Girl breathed a sigh of deep relief.

"A man of his age, though. He's got a bit of money now. I suppose finding companionship among the whores wouldn't be out of the—"

"You're disgusting, Uncle!!"

His continued ruminations brought something welling up from deep within her heart, flushing her face bright red and spilling out her mouth. She tore off her apron and stormed out of the house.

Her uncle caught the apron and was left sitting there, holding it in his hand and looking astonished. Taken aback, he looked from the apron to the wide-open door.

"…"

He fiddled with the apron for a moment, unsure what to do with it; then he looked up at the ceiling and muttered in despair, "…I just can't understand it."

It just didn't make any sense. A girl her age—*Ah, that's it. She's at that age, too.*

"…I suppose prostitutes weren't the wisest topic to bring up."

His bones creaked almost as much as the chair as he rose to his feet and went to the kitchen his niece had just vacated. He checked the fire, then the stew she had been stirring. It was the meal from last night.

"Still…"

That young man belonged on the list of things he didn't understand, too.

He wasn't exactly an unknown. The older man did have a vague memory of having seen him when the boy was young.

And the boy had lived. Become an adventurer. And the old man's niece had some kind of feelings for the boy. All that was well and good.

The problem was…

"…'Goblin Slayer'…?"

The one who killed goblins. The slayer of goblins.

Her uncle had gathered that this was what people were calling the young man now, that he even sometimes used the name himself. He was aware that adventurers frequently gave themselves colorful sobriquets like this in order to promote themselves and their services, but at the same time…

"I hope nothing…odd happens to her…"

The words were out of his mouth before he realized he had spoken. They sounded to him like a father who was afraid his daughter was being seduced by some questionable man, and he frowned. The thought seemed disrespectful to his younger sister and her husband.

§

Goblin Slayer paid for apple cider at the tavern in the Guild building, then hurried down the path, the morning sun shining on him.

"It's already late today," Arc Mage had said. *"Come back tomorrow morning."*

He regretted that he hadn't asked for a specific time. When exactly was "morning"?

After some thought, he decided to go first thing. If he was too early, he could simply wait there.

He was aided by the happy fact that the tavern, which had to serve even the earliest rising of adventurers, was already up and running by that time. The rhea chef was more than pleased to sell him the cider, which now dangled at his hip.

Walking along silently, Goblin Slayer soon arrived at the riverbank. There was the hovel, in the same place it had been the day before.

Despite the ample sunlight, the place felt oddly the same as it had yesterday. The creaking waterwheel was still turning; smoke was still drifting from the chimney. Just a little house. Almost as if it, and it alone, had been clipped out of a bigger picture.

He considered to himself for a second, then walked up to the door and gave several loud, nonchalant raps with the brass knocker.

A voice came from within: "Oh, it's open. Just come in."

Goblin Slayer opened the door and entered to find the place still dim inside. He weaved his way among the piles of junk and the towers of books that blocked the windows.

And there she was: Arc Mage, deep inside, playing with her cards.

"I try not to pile them like that. The humidity from those windows is so bad for the books, you see." Her words had the ring of an excuse. Then she chuckled and turned her chair around. "Does it look like I'm just playing around?" Now facing Goblin Slayer, she fanned the cards out with a flourish. "Such a fine line between sages and idlers! But this is part of my research—I'm compiling a magical treatise."

Arc Mage piled the cards back together, forming a deck. "Now, then." She smiled, cutting the cards. "You're here about your reward. I know I said *morning*, but I didn't expect you quite so early."

"Should I wait?" Goblin Slayer asked, to which she replied, "Nah," with a shake of her head. "Time never stops flowing, after all. For moving things along, early is best."

But—information on goblins? She couldn't restrain more chortles, tears forming in her eyes. "For a newly minted male adventurer all by himself, I might say seventy percent of them say body..."

Goblin Slayer watched as her shoulders began to shake and waited for another one of her fits of laughter to start. She had soon wiped away the tears with her pale fingers, but even so, her lip quivered with amusement.

She gave a great stretch, as if to show herself off, straining against her clothes, making the shape of her body abundantly clear. It was less that she paid no heed to her appearance and more that she didn't need to.

"Speaking of that, that was the one thing I had confidence in as a woman."

"I see."

"As far as the remainder, twenty percent say magical items. And the rest say my knowledge."

"I see."

"...You're an odd one, aren't you?"

"I see."

Goblin Slayer, unsure what to say, simply repeated the same thing each time. Frankly discussing the relations that occurred between men and women no longer flustered him by now, but it did leave him at a loss for how to respond.

Finally, he gave a soft grunt and remained silent. In other words, he decided to do what he always did.

Arc Mage put her chin in her hands, letting out a troubled breath as she shifted her weight. "Aren't you going to ask me what I mean, talking about *bodies* like this?"

"Do you want to be asked?"

"Oh, just ask the question." She opened her arms wide as if looking for a hug.

"Hmm," Goblin Slayer murmured. "What do you mean, talking about bodies like that?"

"I mean I could cast an illusion on you and have all the fun I want, then weave a little spell of forgetfulness and send you home hardly knowing what had happened."

"I see," Goblin Slayer replied, but then a thought took him, and his helmet tilted questioningly. "Isn't that a scam?"

"Value isn't absolute, see—it's relative." Arc Mage's eyes narrowed behind her spectacles; she sounded almost like she was making this up as she went along.

Goblin Slayer thought for a moment, then came to the conclusion that this was pointless.

It reminded him of the riddle games his master had so often played with him. The words themselves had no meaning, no worth. What mattered was figuring out what lay behind those words.

I understand. That is relative indeed.

"In that case," he said, knowing the answer now, setting the jar at his hip on the desk with a plunk, "does this have value? To you, that is."

"I did just get some yesterday, but I could be had. Nothing wrong with keeping a little on hand."

On her desk, the otherwise brand-new bottle was already half empty. Yet, all he smelled was the sweet aroma of apples, not a trace of alcohol in the air. Arc Mage fell into laughter again, not seeming the faintest bit drunk.

©Shingo Adachi

"Goblins, goblins... That's what you wanted to learn, isn't it?"

"That's right."

"Goodness gracious, then you've come at exactly the right time."

Arc Mage swept up the bottle of cider, gave it a little kiss, and then resettled it at the edge of the desk. Then she grabbed a sheaf of sheepskin documents, pointedly clearing away the accumulated dust.

"This slipped my mind for a bit," she said—though he wasn't sure he believed her, and the odor of apples came drifting on her breath—"but as it happens, I've agreed to help revise the Monster Manual."

"..." Goblin Slayer gave this a moment's thought, then asked, "At the Guild's request?"

"Errata and revisions are produced regularly—it's no small job."

Even Goblin Slayer was aware that monsters' ecology sometimes shifted and morphed. It was not possible for humans to record and capture everything there truly was to know about the world. Any sense of understanding was a sort of vanity—though people realized this all too rarely.

"An old master of mine asked for my help. Apparently, they'd been told to get me involved. Me! What a kerfuffle."

"And so what if I write whatever I want? That's what I want to know. Eh? Complain to me, will they?!"

He remembered the aged rhea muttering such things to himself as he scribbled in a notebook.

Goblin Slayer had asked him once what he was writing.

"Poems," came the answer. Then a little needling: *"Do you know how to read a poem, let alone write one?"*

The memories came back unbidden when he heard the word *master*; he chased them away again. Putting together the information he had, Goblin Slayer came to something like a conclusion and quickly voiced it.

"Is it about goblins?"

"Precisely. Goblins, indeed." She gave an exaggerated nod, then leaned over toward Goblin Slayer. She was so close, she could have put her lips on that steel helmet.

Goblin Slayer looked through his visor, into her eyes.

"I want to dissect some goblins, maybe observe them in their natural habitat. And everything I learn, I'll share it immediately with you. That's what I've been thinking." Arc Mage's eyes seemed to glitter behind her spectacles, like the deeps of a rapid river. Her lips formed apple-scented words. "You happen to be something of a specialist in goblin slaying, yes?"

§

It was every bit of it a perfectly ordinary quest.

Goblins, it was said, had appeared outside a small farming village on the frontier. If that had been all, it might have ended there. It had been five years since the great battle. It was hardly unusual to see roving bands of goblins.

But the goblins started ravaging crop fields, then stealing livestock. And when the young men of the village heard that one of their young women had been attacked while doing her chores, they got angry.

There was a man among them who had served in the military and others who had heard from their fathers and grandfathers about combat. They had tools in their sheds; they might have even found some battered old armor if they looked. And they had plenty of hands.

More than enough to chase off the next goblin who came sneaking into the village.

The problems came after that.

The young men, passions inflamed, were eager to mount an assault on the goblin nest. But the village chieftain put a stop to that. There was no need for the youth of his village to do anything dangerous, he said. Hire an adventurer instead...

"You're saying this is typical, then... Practically a template?"

"Yes," Goblin Slayer said. "Although no girls have been kidnapped... But yes."

They were in a forest that was dark even in daytime, talking as they worked their way through the trackless woods.

Goblin Slayer pushed his way through the undergrowth, following the signs the young men had left in their rush a few days before. Arc Mage was holding up the hem of her long robe, though strangely, leaves didn't seem to stick to it. She looked like she was out for a pleasant stroll, apparently having an easier time than Goblin Slayer himself.

I think it's a difference in level, not skill, Goblin Slayer decided as he glanced back at the humming wizard.

Now that he thought about it—did she even have a specific level? And if she did, what was it?

He didn't actually care much, though, so he promptly forgot the question.

Instead, he became aware of continued chattering behind him.

"That would suggest that goblin hordes have a hierarchy of their own."

Arc Mage didn't seem to be speaking to him but rather talking to herself.

"They've only just settled here, right? Wanderers, trying to kidnap a woman. They're looking to expand." As the nest got bigger, the attacks on the village would become more audacious: step two. She counted on her fingers. "And then they would arrive at step three…"

"Destroying the village."

"Yes, that's right." She nodded like an approving instructor. "Demons and evil cultists and dark elves—with every kind of Non-Prayer, you find their path ends up there." As she recited this, Arc Mage brought the jar of alcohol from her hip to her lips. She drank lustily, gave a satisfied *ahhh*, and pulled the bottle away from her mouth with saliva hanging like a silver thread. She licked the last drops from her lips as she said, "Right, then. Is there a stage four?"

"…"

"That's the sort of question I would expect you to ask, but I've never heard of a nest getting big enough to reach that level."

A goblin kingdom. She practically sang the words, but he kept silent and focused on trampling through the brush.

"They're opportunistic, violent little devils. Even if they had a king, I'm sure his kingdom would fracture immediately… Or he'd be assassinated."

"There are adventurers, too," Goblin Slayer said brusquely. He spoke even more quietly than when talking to himself. Then he added, "Most of the time."

"Well, history hasn't seen a perfect government yet. Pray-ers or not." Then Arc Mage chortled happily again.

Shortly thereafter, they arrived at a small hillock nestled in the forest.

No, it wasn't exactly a hillock. It was a grave, covered in earth and ground cover and grown mossy.

A funerary mound—perhaps that would be the right expression.

Maybe it belonged to some ancient king or general, name unknown, tomb now hardly visible.

One lone goblin stood outside the entrance, nominally on patrol, giving a great yawn as he held a spear flecked with red rust...

"Argh, these little beasts don't know the value of what they have," Arc Mage said, her tone considerably lighter than her words. Then she winked at Goblin Slayer. "So what do you think?"

"Hrm." He grunted.

He crouched in the bushes with her, surveying the situation. The goblin was still yawning.

His conclusion was simple.

"We kill him."

"If we wait long enough, someone might replace him, or he might just wander off, right?" Arc Mage glanced up at the canopy of trees, in the general direction of the sun. "Anyway, he looks tired. Maybe they're nocturnal?"

"Possibly." Goblin Slayer took careful note of her words as he checked his weapon over. He reviewed his plan in his mind, confirmed the steps involved, including what he would do in case of failure. No problems anywhere. "But we are going to kill him."

"Why?" Arc Mage almost sounded amused, like she was teasing him.

Goblin Slayer answered without hesitation, "Because eventually, we will kill all the goblins."

"Well, that makes sense."

Show me what you've got, then. By the time the whisper left Arc Mage's lips, Goblin Slayer was already in motion. He steadied his breath, then lunged out of the underbrush and flung his knife.

"GOROGO?!"

Before the goblin could shout anything, he had it screaming with pain from the knife in its shoulder. Goblin Slayer sucked his teeth. He had been aiming for the throat.

He drew his sword and let his momentum carry him forward to drive the blade into the monster's neck.

"GBRROB?! GOB?!"

The goblin choked and frothed blood; and in its flailing, it managed to whack Goblin Slayer's shoulder with the haft of its spear. But he gave a violent twist of his sword, and the goblin's body had one great jerk and stopped moving.

"One."

"Splendid." Arc Mage walked over to him, clapping. He stood beside the body, breathing hard and spattered with blood. "I see the throat is a killing blow. Maybe they aren't so different from people after all. I get the feeling they may be close to rheas."

"I don't know." Goblin Slayer pulled the knife out of the goblin's shoulder and cleaned it off on its loincloth. He also shook the blood from the sword he had used to run through the creature's throat and put it back in its scabbard. Then, finally, he picked up the goblin's spear, checking its quality.

The tip was too rusted to be of any use, but it could serve as a pole. He stuck it into his belt behind his back.

"Sometimes a strike to the throat fails to finish them off."

"Huh. When it's not a critical hit, eh? Very interesting." Arc Mage prodded at the body with her staff, then peeked under the goblin's loincloth and laughed aloud. A moment later, she said, "Right, then," and looked at him cheerfully. "Let's save the dissection for later—time to head into the nest!"

"Right," Goblin Slayer said, but he didn't immediately move. From behind his visor, he fixed Arc Mage with a serious gaze.

"What is it?" she asked with a tilt of her head, smiling alluringly.

"...They may notice a woman's scent."

"Ooh," she said, her eyes shining, evidently unbothered by the possibility that she herself might be a target. "Good smellers, are they? And to think—such filthy creatures, living in these stinky holes."

"There have been times when I'm sure I have not been seen or heard…," Goblin Slayer said, thinking back to the lesson of his first battle. "…But they notice me anyway."

"Well, now." Arc Mage nodded, then suddenly shrugged off her robe. Beneath was a short jacket that revealed a soft line running down to her belly button and a pair of short pants. "Wait just a moment, please."

She tossed the robe to Goblin Slayer, then took a knife full of strange curves from its place at her hip. She drove it into the goblin corpse, slicing open the hideous, protruding belly, and pulled out the innards.

She doused her hands in the dark gore that came pouring forth, covering herself in it as if she were playing in the bath.

"I happen to like that robe, but as for these clothes… Eh." She spun in a circle like a village girl flaunting a bit of tepid fashion. "What do you think?"

"Fine," Goblin Slayer said. Then he added, "I assume."

"Noses are built to filter out the smell of your companions and the other things you encounter routinely." She took the robe back from him, and then, after letting the muck drain off her as much as possible, she put it back on. "For example, you don't notice the smell of fresh leather or new metal, right?"

"No," Goblin Slayer said with a shake of his head. Then he looked at the entrance to the tomb. "But goblins do."

"Precisely!" Arc Mage said as if her point had been made, then she gestured with her staff and a broad grin. "So let's hurry up and get in there!"

Goblin Slayer's only answer was to start walking. Arc Mage followed behind him.

For an instant, it seemed there was a whiff of apples.

No—an olfactory illusion, surely.

It was inconceivable that a goblin nest would smell like anything but goblins.

§

Goblin Slayer peered into the gloom and let out a sigh. He retrieved a torch from his item pouch, striking a flint to light it, then holding it in his left hand, the same side to which his shield was affixed.

"Wouldn't it be better to avoid any light?"

"They have good night vision," he replied to Arc Mage. "I do not."

There was no reason to throw himself headlong into a disadvantageous situation.

"Huh," Arc Mage said, apparently very interested by this, and pursed her lips in thought. "Maybe it's not about *night* vision. It could be that humans and goblins simply see completely different worlds."

She was muttering to herself again. Goblin Slayer listened to her, but he didn't understand.

"Ahh," Arc Mage said when she noticed, laughing. "I guess what matters to you is the point that they can see in the dark. Night or not."

"Is that so?" He took care to remember this. Not night, but dark. It was a major difference.

"Hey, do goblins ever use traps?" Arc Mage asked, looking at the drawings on the walls revealed by the light of the torch. "The previous Monster Manual said a little something about it..."

"Sometimes they've tunneled through to a section of wall behind me," Goblin Slayer answered, scanning the area carefully.

"The sound of frying bacon, huh?"

"...What?"

"Please, carry on."

"..."

He considered how large the tomb had looked to be from the outside, along with where they stood now, the width of the passage, the thickness of the walls. Would goblins be able to break through? He thought about it, but he wasn't yet able to guess. Vigilance would be needed.

"They use pits as well, and sometimes ambushes."

"Simple stuff all around. I guess when you live in a hole, you break down walls and floors... Maybe they could learn to use the traps in ruins, too, through experience..."

"Some assume they couldn't do such a thing... I never have."

"I guess it depends on the living environment. And whether you can learn how those things work from experience. Snowy places, deserts... Different geography means different traps..." Arc Mage was lost in thought again, but then she gave a great laugh. "Not that any of that's going to make it into the book. They use primitive traps. There, done."

Still grinning, she indicated the corpse of some living thing that had been hung up conspicuously. A symbol, put there by the goblins to exemplify the fruits of their killing, eating, and raping.

"You know what wasn't in the book? The stench. How hard it is to walk around here. The claustrophobia, the malice. All the little details."

Goblin Slayer mulled over this for a moment, then said, "I don't think goblins are the only ones like that."

"You're right—I just described the whole book!" she said, then laughed aloud.

Arc Mage's speech had the lyrical flow of music and seemed never to cease. That made Goblin Slayer intensely uneasy. He looked around constantly, straining his ears, trying desperately to catch the slightest sound.

He heard noises and voices belonging to something other than himself and the goblins, felt the presence of it. Something was moving.

Am I getting distracted?

No, no. It just meant there were one or two more things he had to pay attention to.

He took a deep breath, filling his lungs with the fetid, dank air, then slowly released it. Some kind of sticky filth clung to his boots and seemed likely to make noise when he walked. He would have to be careful.

Come to think of it, it seemed he could hardly hear the footsteps of the woman with him…

"Hmm?" Suddenly, cut off by a sound of surprise from Arc Mage, the torrent of words stopped, and Goblin Slayer stopped with them.

"What's wrong?"

"Look at this," she said, gesturing at the muck at their feet with her staff. "It's animal dung."

Goblin Slayer knelt down, unhesitatingly reaching into the stuff with his glove-clad hand.

He remembered this shape. His older sister had taught him about it long ago, when he was small.

"It doesn't appear to belong to a goblin…"

"No, definitely not. It's probably…" She trailed off, looking down the passageway, into the tomb. Belatedly, Goblin Slayer brought up the torch.

The walls and floor, but not the ceiling, glittered in the light, almost as if they had a wire frame on them.

And then from far away came an echo, a faint sound. It sounded like…

"It's from a wolf," Arc Mage said.

The sound was the howl of an animal.

"Do you know any spells?" Goblin Slayer asked quietly.

"Can't have you underestimating me," Arc Mage replied. "I would hate for you to think wizards can't do anything but fling fireballs and call down thunderbolts. But then again…" The electric magus started shuffling the deck of cards she'd taken out of her item pouch and laughed as if the whole thing were a giant joke to her. "…I'm the quest giver today. It's your job to do something about this, not mine."

"I see…!"

The light now revealed two wolves, yowling as they came closer, splattering through the filth. There had been no fork in the path to this point. They would have to meet the creatures head-on. Hiding was impossible.

Letting these thoughts continue to run in a corner of his mind, Goblin Slayer immediately brought up the torch in his left hand. There was a clang as he swept aside the first wolf, which had leaped at him, slamming it into the wall.

Goblin Slayer used the torch he had as a club, meanwhile drawing his sword with his other hand.

"Hrgh…?!"

But the wolf won out in speed and body mass. He slashed the creature from shoulder to chest, but its thick pelt kept the wound from being fatal. The momentum of the monster's charge sent Goblin Slayer sprawling backward. His sword fell from his hand, clattering to the stone floor, and grime splashed up under his steel helmet.

Fangs ripe with the stench of flesh gnashed inches away from his throat.

If it reaches my neck, I'm done for...!

Without hesitation, Goblin Slayer let go of the torch, bringing his shield around to deflect the fangs.

The animal who had been slammed into the wall had regained its footing and was coming his way as well. There was no time.

He gave up any thought of retrieving his sword, instead reaching for the spear at his back.

"Take...this...!"

He worked the rotten haft like a lever, splitting it in two, and then he grabbed it in a reverse grip, shoving the butt end into the wolf's eye.

A howl. The creature's feet were scrambling to back away, but he grabbed them, mashing the eyeball further with the spear. Digging into the brain.

"......Next!"

He shoved aside the frothing, twitching wolf and stood up. The other animal jumped at him, saliva running from its mouth.

Goblin Slayer ducked low and rolled forward, passing under the creature. He grabbed the torch off the ground with his left hand as he went.

"Hrr—ahh...!"

He turned around again, jamming the torch into the wolf's belly. The creature yelled, and there was the rancid smell of burning flesh and fur.

A torch was not, of course, intended to serve as a weapon. The flame promptly went out.

Goblin Slayer, though, shoved the still-glowing stick into the wolf's mouth, dealing the final blow despite the extinguished flame.

"Very nice. A well-judged fight."

"The real mission is still to come." Steadying his breathing, Goblin Slayer picked up his sword. From his item pouch, he produced another torch, which went into his left hand, same as before.

"*Arma...inflammarae...offero.* Gift a spark to weapons." Unexpectedly, there was a sound of fingers snapping, and then a spit of flame.

The glowing fire darted through the air and connected with the torch, setting it alight.

Arc Mage tapped the floor of the disgusting goblin nest with the heel of her long boot, then smiled. "In the name of red magic. Now go ahead and keep protecting your quest giver, my little Goblin Slayer."

"Very good," Goblin Slayer said briefly, then he settled into a fighting posture, preparing for the army whose steps he could hear thundering down the hallway.

The cheap-looking steel helmet, the grimy leather armor, the torch and the sword of a strange length in his hands, the small round shield on his arm.

"The goblins—I'm going to kill them all."

The battle began.

§

"GOROB! GOROBG!"

"GOOROGGB!!"

It's an adventurer. A pitiful, weak-looking adventurer. And a woman, too. Kill! Rape!

The goblins rushed forward, a panoply of crude weapons in their hands, filthy saliva dangling from their mouths.

Goblin Slayer met them in the narrow corridor.

"Two… Three!"

"GGB?!"

"GOROG! GBBGB?!"

Keeping Arc Mage behind him, he deflected a rusty dagger against his shield, then struck back with his sword. He kicked aside the first still-twitching corpse, into the path of the second oncoming goblin. Then in the same motion, he threw his weapon at a third lol-lygagging monster.

"GBGB?!"

"Four—five!"

He pulled out the dagger that had lodged in his shield, slamming it into the skull of the third goblin, who was just clearing the corpse with evident annoyance. This enemy fell over, limbs flailing; Goblin Slayer swept up his club and used it in like manner against the fourth charging monster.

"GOROGORB?!"

Including the first guard, that made five.

A little swinging of weaponry and bashing with a shield, though, wasn't going to slow down the goblins.

"Boy, what a show of force! I'm afraid I might fall in love, here." Arc Mage, who had come up to get a look at the fighting, said something unthinkable, and then cackled loudly. "Relying on numbers, though? Very goblin-esque but not very sophisticated— Whoops!"

She sounded like a theatergoer surprised by a twist in the plot.

"GOROGB!"

"GBB! GROGOB!"

Goblin Slayer gave a click of his tongue. Those goblin voices were coming from behind. So the brood had circled around, flanking them through the entrance!

"Makes sense. They couldn't tunnel through the walls here, but they achieve the same thing this way. Wonder if they had a back door."

"Stand with your back to the wall!" he shouted.

"Oh sure," Arc Mage replied and dutifully turned. Goblin Slayer stood in front of her.

In his right hand, he held a club, in his left, a torch. He held out his arms, menacing the goblins on either side. If there was no attack from behind, this would allow him to protect her—at least as long as he survived.

"Six!"

"GOBOGOR?!"

Holding the goblin to his right at bay with the club, he clubbed the goblin to his left with the torch. The magical flame crackled and engulfed the goblin's head, burning it to a crisp.

"GGGOB?!"

"Like it? I told you there was more to us than simply flinging fireballs."

Enchant Fire.

Goblin Slayer had no special interest in the names of the spells she could incant. Kicking aside the screaming, writhing goblin, he immediately transferred the flame of the torch to his club.

Now with two burning weapons, Goblin Slayer began lashing out at monsters left and right.

"Seven... Eight! Nine! ...Ten!"

Right, left. Each time he swung one of the burning brands, a trail of sparks followed, a glowing arc hovering in the air.

Magical weapons were not necessary for killing goblins—but arcane fire, that was more than enough to give them pause. The monsters didn't know what to do in the face of the roaring, flaming weapons but continued to lash out mercilessly.

"GGGBGOR?!"

"GOB?! GGOBOGOG?!"

There was the smell of frying goblin flesh, the stink of boiling blood, and brains and bits of skull flying everywhere.

"It's an awfully excessive spell to cast on a club, though..."

Goblin Slayer heard Arc Mage's murmur at the same time as the flame on his club disappeared.

He had killed well more than ten goblins already, and the tide of monsters was beginning to ebb.

Goblin Slayer let out a deep breath. His shoulders heaved, and he wiped sweat from his eyes: He was alive. She was safe.

He could see, though, that his torch and club had reached their limits; he nonchalantly tossed them down at his feet. In their place, he trod on the fingers of one of the corpses, taking the sturdiest-looking sword available.

He worked hard to control his breathing as he asked, "...How many more?"

Endurance, physical strength, was not a problem to be solved in one fell swoop—but now more than ever, he felt keenly the need to continue to train.

"Good question," Arc Mage replied cheerfully. "Considering the villagers' accounts and the number of footprints we saw by the entrance, I'd have to guess we're about through." She sat down on a piece of rock wall that had come loose, and she chuckled. "You're quite the fighter, though. I'm afraid I really might fall in love with you."

"I see."

"You're hard to get a rise out of."

"I would not want to take you seriously if you were joking."

"If I couldn't throw someone into a tizzy with just a few words, well, I wouldn't be quite sure what to do with myself... Oops, here they come."

Of course, Goblin Slayer didn't need her to tell him that; he heard it, too. Heavy, dull footsteps, *bum, bum*. They were coming closer through the ruins, and they sounded like something he had heard just the other day.

A massive form filled the passageway—but that wasn't all. At the form's feet hid a slithering shadow.

"A hob, and..."

"...Ah-ha, one of those shamans. This nest was on its way to reaching stage two, I see."

The giant goblin looked absolutely idiotic. The one by his feet held a staff and looked considerably more intelligent.

He didn't know which of them was the leader. But he was sure that he was at last facing the chieftain of the horde.

"I guess that means the decoration earlier was a totem of some kind," Arc Mage murmured, realization dawning.

Goblin Slayer didn't really understand. He was paying attention to something else.

The hobgoblin had a "shield" in his hand.

The shield was in the form of a person. Like a doll with its hands and legs bent in obscene directions.

"Ah... Ee..."

There hadn't been any reports of captured village women. She must be a wanderer, then, or perhaps a traveler. The hobgoblin thrust his shield about as if showing the woman off. She cried out as her breasts were smashed into the wall.

The goblins cackled. This wasn't about their dead companions; they were making fun of the pathetic condition of the shield, and these adventurers who were surely no threat to them.

"......"

"Well, isn't that awful," Arc Mage said as if it hardly concerned her. "I wonder if she's pregnant. Gosh, I sure wouldn't mind getting a look at that baby."

Goblin Slayer ignored her, steadying his breathing. He slowly rotated his sword in his hand.

The world wavered. He held his breath. Fixed his aim. Lowered his arm. Just the slightest bit.

He had learned something from the fight earlier.

They don't know how to use shields.

"GOROGOBOGOR?!?!"

The goblin—the hobgoblin—gave an earsplitting screech. The monster didn't understand what had happened to him, but no doubt he wouldn't have believed it had he known. He never would have believed that a sword had been stabbed into his exposed thigh, which he couldn't hide behind his shield...

"Hrrr—ahh!" Goblin Slayer reached behind himself with his right hand, pulled out the broken spear, and jumped in. The goblin shaman, aware of the hobgoblin's shameful mistake, jabbered and waved his staff.

"GOBOOGOB...!"

"Spell incoming!" Arc Mage shouted. It was all right. He knew.

"GOROOOGOB?!"

"Heeek...?!"

The hobgoblin sent his captive spinning through the air; Goblin Slayer caught her. She was light. This wouldn't stop his momentum. He jumped in, deep, wielding the spear in one hand.

"Ten—and one!!"

"GOBOOROG?! GOBOG?!"

He closed the distance, not worried what he hit so long as it would stop the spell. The mouth and tongue. Crush the throat. The rusty spear tip all but shattered as it lodged in the shaman's windpipe. The monster howled.

Goblin Slayer kicked aside the creature choking on its own blood and turned toward the hobgoblin.

"GORGGBBBB...!"

"This is twelve...!"

He held nothing in his hands. But there was a weapon right in front of him.

Zigging and zagging, Goblin Slayer ducked in and kicked the flailing hobgoblin in the crotch.

"GOOBBGBGRGBG?!"

And there was the sword, too, of course.

It buried itself up to the hilt; he could feel the soft sensation of internal organs giving way.

But I know that's not enough to kill you.

"GOROGBB?!?!"

He laid the prisoner on the ground and set upon the writhing hobgoblin. The shield on his left arm came around. It might have been easier if he'd honed it more. He felt some regret at that.

The metal edge smashed deep into the hobgoblin's skull. Then another blow. Brains came flying out.

A few twitches followed and nothing more. The tremor of the death rattle set the thick limbs stiff.

And that was the end.

§

The fire crackled and sparked, smoke drifting along with the awful smell in the air. The stench in the dim ruins was even more stomach-turning than before.

"Here's the stomach, and here's the small intestine... But I guess you knew that, didn't you?"

"Yes."

"This is where food is digested. Here's the bladder and the testicles. A man's...you know. That's a vital point."

Arc Mage had a cloth over her mouth and was using a blade curved like a cat's claw to perform an autopsy.

"Don't know if this one's big or small." She sounded like she was making a joke, but Goblin Slayer listened intently.

Lying in front of them was a goblin, his abdomen torn cruelly open and his guts spilled out. He wasn't the only one; several of the other goblin corpses had been likewise disemboweled.

"Now that's enough to make a woman cry." Arc Mage chuckled, plucking at the goblin's member with her fingers. "It looks like it's true they don't have any females, though. Nobody in this whole crowd has a womb or eggs."

The battle had ended, and the sun had gone down, bringing on the night, which was the goblins' time. Should he really have let the woman wearing the apron covered with congealed goblin blood do such a leisurely dissection? Goblin Slayer was still wondering that even as both of them sat surrounded by viscera.

"If there are any left, they might come back," Arc Mage had said, but strangely enough, she was the one who suggested they pitch camp there for the night.

Goblin Slayer still found her reasoning difficult to fathom. Did she want to hurry up and do the dissections before any remaining goblins came back, or was her plan to do the work while waiting to ambush any returnees…?

"We sure don't want her to get attacked by goblins again, do we?" A chuckle. She indicated the girl, who had been given first aid, wrapped in a blanket, and then magically put to sleep.

Whatever the case, this was preferable to being attacked while moving, trying to carry both goblin corpses and an unconscious former captive. All Goblin Slayer could do was nod, and after that, there was only one course of action.

"Help me with the dissection, please." Arc Mage's movements were preternaturally smooth and graceful. Her eyes reflected a cat-like glint as she performed the operation, her pale fingertips becoming stained with dark cruor.

"The position of the liver and kidneys isn't so different from in a human," she said. "Can't speak to the internal structure of other races, though."

"I see."

"You know how rarely you get a chance to dissect an elf or a dwarf? And rhea thieves never seem to hang themselves, either." She rooted through the goblin's guts with a kind of compassionate artlessness, pulling out the liver. "Land a hit here, and it really hurts; give it a good stab, and it bleeds all over. You'd need a miracle to save you."

"…In the past, goblins have sometimes kept on going even though I stabbed them in the stomach," Goblin Slayer said, voicing a question he'd had for a long time. "Why is that?"

"Toughness… Or maybe I should say, hit points."

Arc Mage diligently pointed out that she couldn't be sure without seeing it for herself, before she started speaking. They hadn't known each other very long, but she seemed to be someone who willingly admitted when she didn't understand things and wouldn't spout off about things she didn't know. That was a quality for which Goblin Slayer was immensely grateful. There was little more frustrating than trusting ill-founded advice and then feeling like a fool.

If you're going to dine with long-lost relatives, do your research on them first, his master had told him.

"Sometimes you hit a vital point, but they don't die instantly," Arc Mage said. "Or perhaps it's that the blade is stopped by muscle or fat and never reaches the spot necessary to deal a killing blow."

"That makes sense." Goblin Slayer touched the sword that served him so faithfully (though he didn't think of it in those terms). It was disposable, of a strange length. Too short to use on the battlefield proper, too long to cart around everywhere simply for personal protection. Exactly the right size for killing goblins in enclosed spaces—but perhaps he should try to avoid stabbing the big ones with it…?

But stabbing was a much more certain kill than slashing. He would be foolish to ignore what was proven to work.

"Where should I aim?"

"Hmm. Just a moment, please." Arc Mage sounded like he had placed an order at a restaurant. She began digging through the goblin corpse again.

Watching her, he realized how rough and unrefined his own earlier dissections had been. The presence of specialist knowledge and techniques made itself known in the little details. Goblin Slayer fixed his eyes on her and listened attentively so that none of those experienced movements or words would escape him.

"……Okay, there are major arteries in the thigh, under the armpit, and in the neck. The respiratory tract is approximately the same as in people, too. Those are your targets."

"The neck… Throat?" Goblin Slayer nodded and thought about this. Destroy the throat. It had worked before. The effect was obvious. But he also remembered how the knife he'd thrown at the guard had missed. It was clear what he had to do.

"I will need to practice."

"Heh-heh. Speaking of being similar to people, *and* practicing…"

Arc Mage gave him a pointed glance, then walked into the gloom of the ruins. Her come-hither look led him to a pile of junk. Perhaps they were funerary offerings of some kind; among them were many rust-eaten weapons that looked like they would shatter if they were used to stab anything. Among them, though, was something of patchy, unsightly leather, something discovered deep within the nest.

"A saddle," Arc Mage breathed. "Who would have expected?"

Goblin Slayer received these words expressionlessly.

Goblin riders.

The goblins had been keeping those wolves as mounts.

"…Does this, too, go back to that battle five years ago?"

"Nobody knows whether they saw other races doing it, or if someone taught them. But somehow, goblins learned the art of riding." Arc Mage pulled the cloth away from her mouth, carefully wiping her hands and cleaning them with alcohol. Then she rested her elbows on her knees and her chin in her hands and narrowed her eyes as she looked at Goblin Slayer. "All living things respond to the environment in which they live."

Her gaze was profoundly strange, as if she were watching a bug. She seemed both intrigued and not the least interested in what would become of the subject of her observation…

"Did you know? Humans who live in cold places come to have bigger bodies. Like the barbarian of the north."

"…I've heard stories." Goblin Slayer thought back to the bedtime tales his older sister used to tell him.

The barbarian of the north. A man of bravery. A warrior and a pirate. All the many adventures he had, all the treasures he pillaged and thrones he overthrew. How with nothing but his sword in his hand, he rose from slave to mercenary to general, and finally to king, a great man in a great tale.

To Goblin Slayer, this story was history, and myth, and legend, and also a bedtime story. It meant nothing to him whether it had happened or not. It meant nothing to him who might mock him for it.

For to him, this heroic tale was the truth.

"They were the ones who offered steel."

"Exactly." Arc Mage nodded, removing her apron with a casual motion and letting it fall to the ground. She plopped herself down beside the bonfire, patting the ground beside her, inviting him over.

"You know it?" Goblin Slayer said softly, as if he couldn't believe what he had heard.

"The desolate darkness and the country of night. The way he cursed the people who mocked him for simple machismo, never knowing his true splendor."

Yes, that's right. Goblin Slayer nodded. Then after a moment's thought, he seated himself next to the still-sleeping captive, across from Arc Mage.

She watched him. "That's all well and good," she said with a thin smile, and then she looked into the flames. "But there's something my master told me... Something the lizardmen say. That long, long ago, there was an age of tremendous cold."

That's the legend. She didn't really speak the words, just formed them with her lips.

"And they claim goblins have existed from at least that time—so these hobgoblins, as you call them, might just be creatures who went back to their roots."

Goblin Slayer looked over at the corpse lying at a distance from the fire. It was the massive goblin he had slain after such struggle—the hobgoblin. It hardly even looked like a goblin, and he had given it little further thought, but...

"You're suggesting the muscles are so large simply due to a change in body shape...?"

"It's possible. It might mean the goblins' ancestors roamed freely across the plains, rather than living in caves." Arc Mage brought the bottle of cider to her lips and suckled at it, then took a loud swig. "Goblins *do* come out into the field to attack villages when they're strong enough...don't they?"

"…" Goblin Slayer grunted softly, then nodded. "Sometimes."

"That might imply the state of their nutrition has an impact. Who knows what might happen if they got regular, decent food?"

Goblin Slayer was silent. He couldn't imagine.

Filthy goblins eating like humans, leading lives like humans. It was a terrible thought.

Even in regions controlled by the forces of Chaos, goblins were but the lowliest of foot soldiers. That fact wouldn't change until the day goblins overthrew every one of those who had words in the four corners of the world.

Goblins made nothing for themselves—they pilfered and stole everything.

"Oh, say, do you know about that research into fish bodies and schools?" Arc Mage never stopped talking. Goblin Slayer was forced to think about the next thing.

"I don't." He replied to the unexpected question with detachment. There was no reason to be flustered. It was better than having rocks thrown at you while you tried to answer a riddle. "I've never heard of it."

"I don't blame you." Arc Mage nodded and continued, "I heard about it from my master. They say if you compare fish who travel in schools with fish who live alone, the ones on their own get bigger."

"…That sounds like common sense to me."

"Scholarship is all about investigating 'common sense.' Otherwise, you'll never get past the common." Arc Mage sounded rather pleased with herself. She puffed out her ample chest and smiled. "In overcrowded schools, growth is retarded, and the water becomes polluted with excrement. The fish become incensed and readily resort to cannibalism…"

"…"

"Basically, they become goblins. See what I'm saying?"

Goblin Slayer, still not speaking, watched the wood as it cracked on the fire. He could feel Arc Mage's smile on him, as if she could see straight through his helmet.

But so what? Goblin Slayer said, "…The way you speak sounds strange to me."

"I told you, my master was a lizardman. And I was his student. A top-flight heretic of a pupil, in other words." Arc Mage peered at the fire through her bottle, then licked a few drops off the lip. "Lizardmen hate to leave any written records, though. So I've had to remember everything.

"Rheas write however they like, dwarves don't fancy talk, and elves stop short at 'It's only natural.'

"Immortal wizards merely write themselves some notes—their brains are rotting away."

So she went on, smiling and talking what seemed to be nonsense, but he only interjected the occasional "I see."

"Dragons, you know, they can remember everything without writing it down. And they never die, so they never forget."

Goblin Slayer stirred the fire with a nearby stick and replied, "I see."

"I'll bet you do," Arc Mage said, chuckling deep in her throat. "Dragons love to hoard. Knowledge is a lot like treasure for them. They don't share it with anyone without a price." Arc Mage began humming to herself. Some sparks flew, adding their crackles to the music.

Knowledge is a treasure.

Look, behold the sage here in this cave. Look how much knowledge is demanded of this wizard-sage to inscribe just one page of a book.

"But at the same time, if you kill them, the knowledge vanishes. The sneakiest burglar in all of existence can't possibly get inside a dragon's head."

Goblin Slayer suddenly found himself thinking about his own master, the old rhea.

"Why should I go out of my way to teach some cast-off piece of filth who's only going to be killed by goblins?!"

Thus, his master had exclaimed, and then beaten him harshly about his worthless head.

He had no treasure to offer a fool with no learning, an idiot whose only possession was a simple confidence that he would be victorious.

Perhaps, he thought, Arc Mage's master, the lizardman, had

himself been a dragon, a naga. But his interest went no further than that; it didn't even occur to him to ask her about it.

"But if you *could* get a dragon to share his knowledge with you…" Her cheeks looked slightly red, but he couldn't tell whether it was from the cider or just the glow of the flames. Her gaze seemed soft, though, as it rested on his helmet. "…If you had that chance, and you told him you wanted to know about goblins? That would make you a weird guy, indeed."

"I see," Goblin Slayer said. The conversation lapsed again.

The fire sparked as another log broke. Goblin Slayer strained his ears, but he didn't hear any goblin footsteps. All he heard was his own muffled breathing and the quiet inhale-exhale of his companion. The even breaths of the sleeping woman.

The only thing he sensed was the sweet smell of apples mixed in among the stench of filth and blood and viscera.

Eventually, Arc Mage broke the silence. "Anyway, I guess the things to study are biology, behavior, origins, subspecies, habitat, knowledge, intelligence, and culture, and that about covers it." She sounded impossibly cheerful. "Not that I'm eager to study any more than that on my own. Like…language, say. Goblinese…

"Think there's such a thing?" It was a teasing question, one she'd voiced several times over the past several days.

"There is," Goblin Slayer said flatly. There was no room for argument in his mind.

"You sure about that? They might just be animalistic cries. I know the *gob-gob* stuff sounds like they're talking, but you never know."

But he didn't have to hear them to know. He had known it for five years now.

"I saw them pointing at captives, laughing and mocking them."

"So goblin culture includes humor, is what you're saying." Arc Mage nodded happily, once again adopting the tone of a professor praising a distinguished student.

Goblin Slayer, unable to parse exactly what she meant, fell into a sullen silence.

Through his visor, he could see that Arc Mage seemed unconcerned; she just kept talking. "Aw, what's the matter? That's a new discovery! One of those hard-earned nuggets of goblin knowledge you're so eager for."

"…Is that so?"

"Uh-huh. Research—about anything, not just monsters—is really the slow accumulation of experimental results."

The *Draconomicon*, the *Demonicon*, or, from an alternative angle, *A Guide to Skaven*.

"I'm not interested," Goblin Slayer said, again without hesitation.

Why? Arc Mage barely voiced the word. "Finding out where goblins came from might give you a better idea about how to fight them."

He calmly gave her the reply he had settled on many years ago. "Because while I was doing that, goblins would be destroying villages."

"—"

It was Arc Mage's turn to be silent. To Goblin Slayer, it looked as if she had been struck dumb. But his responses were already set. They had been for five years—no, indeed, for much longer than that.

"Also," he went on, "I already know where goblins come from. The green moon."

He offered nothing further. His older sister had told him this. And his older sister was never wrong about anything.

"It was her. She taught me."

"…" Arc Mage didn't have an immediate answer. She drank her cider, wiped her lips, and then looked down, away from the bonfire. "Planeswalking, is that it?"

It was a mysterious word. Wizards' words always were.

And she looked so tense—the smile that made its way onto her face seemed somehow forced.

"That's just a made-up story, a fairy tale to frighten children. And for adults to chuckle at… Isn't it?"

"I have never found it amusing."

"…"

That was the last of the conversation until dawn broke. Arc Mage didn't breathe another word, nor did Goblin Slayer speak to her.

At last, the first light of the morning sun cast itself among the stones. When the pale beam had slithered up to his feet like a snake, Goblin Slayer stood up.

There were no more goblins here. He had killed them all. The only thing left to do was to go back to the village, return the girl to them, and then go home.

He started walking, the girl supported on his back, and Arc Mage followed silently behind him. They left the ruins to find the sunlight piercing through gaps in the forest canopy, stinging their eyes like needles. Goblin Slayer squinted behind the visor of his helmet and began walking slowly through the woods.

"Darkness everlasting." Two short words came unexpectedly from behind him, from Arc Mage. "Past the edge of this table, beyond the void, on the far side of eternity, the unending search."

None of the things she was saying made any sense to Goblin Slayer. She sounded oddly sad, lonely almost, but he felt no special interest in this, either.

"Well, to travel is to have traveling companions… But I guess we aren't all going to the same place anyway."

He wasn't interested, and so he made no special effort to remember this conversation any more than any of the others.

"…Erghh."

She was well aware she couldn't outright say this was boring, but she couldn't stop herself from letting out a sigh.

The Adventurers Guild, just after noon. It was full of the flaccid indolence of the hour when lunch break had just ended.

Guild Girl's sharp-eared colleague was quick to interrogate the receptionist where she lay stretched out on the front desk.

"What is it? What's going on?"

"Nothing's going on."

The other woman's eyes seemed awfully eager, for a follower of the Supreme God.

Guild Girl didn't want to be part of these games. She turned pointedly away.

"Ah-ha." Her colleague laughed. "This is about your favorite novice!"

"Ergh…"

Bingo.

She was so on target that Guild Girl seriously wondered whether she might have used the Inspiration miracle. She was fairly sure that gift came from the God of Knowledge, but still…

"Hasn't he been in touch recently?"

"…What's that supposed to mean?" Guild Girl grimaced at her

colleague, who was smirking like a cat toying with a mouse. What was she implying—that Guild Girl was waiting with bated breath for him to come back?

"Well, it's all good, right? Adventurers have their own lives." Her colleague laughed. Where they fought, where they died. They were the ones who got to choose.

"I know that," Guild Girl replied, her expression growing more sour by the word. "He's completed all his assignments flawlessly, as usual. I guess he's been busy helping that wizard lately."

"Ahh, so that's what this is about."

Oops. Fumble.

Her friend's grin got a little wider, and Guild Girl mentally jumped to take back what she had said.

Surely this shouldn't have been so worrisome. Adventurers took all kinds of jobs and had their preferred quest givers. That was something to celebrate, wasn't it?

But it was just, you know... How could she put it?

It makes me...depressed.

Arc Mage—she was the spell caster who lived in the wheelhouse on the edge of town. A mad wizard, or perhaps a sage.

Guild Girl was aware Arc Mage had taken *him* on as a research assistant, and that he frequently went to her house.

In fact, it was Guild Girl who had given him the quest in the first place. She herself. Yes, but...

Hey, they look like a good match.

When she started hearing things like that around, she felt herself growing depressed for some reason.

These were adventurers, people who didn't know what tomorrow would bring. Idle chatter—romantic gossip, or simple dirty stories—was one of their pleasures. Of course they would talk thoughtlessly about such things, and it would do her no good to prickle at every one of them. Especially considering she had introduced the two of them.

She hated the feeling of selfishness it produced in her. After all, she was in no special relationship with him.

That's right: he was an adventurer, and she was a receptionist at

the Adventurers Guild, and that was all. How self-absorbed of her to see it as anything to fret and worry and get envious over.

I mean...

Goblin Slayer. The adventurer who had come to be called by that name was obsessed, talking of nothing but goblins.

There had to be something wrong with him. The nickname came about all too naturally, Guild Girl reflected. She was probably in the minority, having talked to this character a bit, having come to have some acquaintance with him.

So who was this Arc Mage—this person who seemed to have gotten so close to him in such a short time?

Guild Girl had heard Arc Mage had been requested to help with the revision of the Monster Manual. She'd heard she was the disciple of a fairly famous mage.

She was certainly researching something, pursuing something. Most wizards were. But the rumors that she was fixated on the Scales of the Twelve Knights that had ended the Summer of the Dead... Those couldn't be true.

Scales as such were perfectly ordinary items. It was only the knights who found those scales who were truly distinguished. Even the story that she was searching for the Ancestral Bird of Paradise had more credence.

Whatever the truth, Guild Girl knew little about him and less about her. That was probably the simplest way to explain the gloom in her heart...

"Eh, feel better," her colleague said when she saw her, chuckling and giving her a gentle pat on the back. "You and I are good for more than just saying, '*Welcome to the Adventurers Guild! How can I help you?*'"

"But isn't that our job?"

"We work to live, right?"

"Well, sure, I guess."

"Then enjoy yourself! Worry, love, live!"

"Love..."

Guild Girl found herself smiling bitterly. This colleague of hers—this friend—was a bit too eager.

Too eager?

She felt her own cheeks flush. She hadn't yet been able to put that name to the feeling in her heart.

"'Scuse me."

It was at that moment when the door clattered open, and somebody sidled up toward the counter at a walking pace.

Guild Girl blinked.

A grimy robe was hiding the person's face, and they gave off a strange aura, as if somehow removed from the scene around them.

"There's a little something I'd like to ask for. Something I might need soon."

When Arc Mage said this to her, Guild Girl discovered she could only nod and reply "Yes?"

"I'm going out."

"Oh, okay…"

Cow Girl kept herself from asking *Already?* as she watched him walk out into the predawn gloom.

No conversation, again. No breakfast, again. And of course, no dinner the night before.

I'm glad he's started coming home, but…

Cow Girl let out a melancholy sigh and leaned across the table, her great chest pressing into it. He sometimes slept in his room now. She sensed it wasn't quite the same as when they had just been reunited. But still…

Maybe I'm only bothering him, pushing things on him like this.

She couldn't stop the thought from crossing her mind.

Something was strange, there was no question. Something crucial—he had done more than simply become an adventurer, she suspected.

Cow Girl went to the Guild sometimes herself. So she heard the things people said.

Goblin Slayer. The one who kills goblins.

Why? She hardly had to ask.

What she wanted to know instead was, what could she do for him?

She remembered riding in that carriage as she left the village, looking back. The evening before, she had argued with him, making him cry, crying herself.

The faces of her mother and father were already painfully blurry in her mind.

She remembered the empty coffins they had buried.

In the midst of all these reminiscences, one thing she had no memories of was her village, ravaged by goblins.

No memories at all.

Instead there was just a blank space, like the spot on the beach where a sandcastle she had worked hard to build had been washed away.

"………*Sigh.*"

Was she just butting in?

Cow Girl let her head roll to one side, taking in the kitchen. There was a pot full of stew, waiting to grow warm.

That time, the time when he had come home practically in tatters, she thought he had eaten it politely.

But maybe she had just imagined it. Maybe it was just what she had wanted to see.

"…Guess I don't know."

Not about him. Not about adventuring.

Dawn broke as she sat thinking these thoughts. The light grew brighter outside. Soon her uncle would be awake.

"…Gotta get Uncle's breakfast ready."

"Perhaps he has a lover somewhere. Or finding companionship among the whores wouldn't be out of the—"

"……!"

At the memory of her uncle's words, she sat up fast enough to rattle the table.

Her face was hot. So hot. She must be bright red. Cow Girl quickly shook her head.

"I th-think I'll go wash my face…!"

She ran out the door, face still burning, and then—

"…Huh?"

She stopped at an unexpected sight. The fence, the one she had told herself she had better fix, had a hasty patch on it.

"…?"

Cow Girl thought about it for a moment, came to the conclusion that her uncle must have fixed it, then continued running to the well.

§

There was the little house, standing just where it always was. The waterwheel creaked along, and smoke puffed from the chimney. A small place.

Morning mist, the color of milk, floated around as Goblin Slayer strode boldly up to the door. He gave a few solid raps of the knocker and was met by a voice that called "Come on in."

He opened the door and entered the room made dim by towers of books. He worked his way through the space, careful not to topple the piles of stuff that looked to him like junk, but whose purpose he didn't know.

"Hey, sorry. Little busy here."

In the very back of the veritable cavern, Arc Mage sat working industriously at her desk. Her fingers moved the cards quick as magic, the little slips becoming blurs as if she were performing sleight of hand.

"I brought cider."

"Great. Just leave it over there somewhere."

She didn't even look in his direction; Goblin Slayer obediently put the bottle down in an arbitrary spot.

Several empty bottles rolled at his feet, a sweet aroma drifting up from them. A mingling of apples and herbs—her smell.

"Also, I have the item you requested." Goblin Slayer dug in his item pouch, producing a small hempen bag. Its mouth was cinched tightly shut, but even so, a faint unpleasant odor drifted through the room. To be fair, that might have had something to do with the grime that was covering him...

"Goblin droppings."

"Great. Just leave it over there somewhere."

She sounded totally disinterested, but it didn't seem to bother him; he simply nodded and set the pouch down in an arbitrary spot.

For the past several days, it had been the same routine.

Goblins were not to be afforded many pages in the Monster Manual.

But that, according to Arc Mage, didn't excuse them from doing their research before writing. So he would collect some goblin-related item and deliver it to her. Then he would receive a reward.

No matter where he put it down, the next time he visited, the item was always gone. None of this was any problem in his mind.

"My reward?"

"Ahh, right. Good point."

An ambiguous response. Goblin Slayer waited patiently for the next words. He looked at her small back for a few moments, and then finally she said, "Ah," as if just remembering. "There's some scrolls over there. You can take one."

She sounded as if she were foisting something on him that she didn't need, but he simply replied, "All right."

He looked "over there" as he'd been instructed, and indeed, there was a collection of neatly rolled scrolls piled together.

"It doesn't matter which I take?"

"Doesn't matter."

"Hmm," he said and thought a moment, then grabbed the topmost scroll, so as not to disturb the pile.

The scroll seemed to be on sheepskin. It had a simple binding and was kept shut with a decorative cord tied in a strange sort of knot.

A magic scroll, presumably. This was the first time Goblin Slayer had ever seen one.

"What's this?"

"Just ask some wizard in town what's in it," Arc Mage said, and then she seemed to forget about him entirely.

One after another, cards turned over, danced upon the tabletop, front and back changing position at dizzying speeds, until finally they were stacked up. On her flashing fingers shone the light of that ring. It still seemed to burn from within.

Goblin Slayer watched it for a moment, then told her he was leaving and exited the room.

Just as the door closed, he heard her say, "See you later." It was just a politeness.

Most likely.

§

"…What, is it?"

Goblin Slayer was at the tavern; the curt question came at him from Witch. She was in a seat in one corner of the room, her staff leaning against the wall; she herself had her legs crossed regally, relaxing. She was eye-catching indeed, and other adventurers glanced their way periodically.

There must have been a great many adventurers who tried to talk to this rookie, a woman and a wizard who ran solo. But the gazes would avert again when they saw who was standing across from her: the man in the grimy armor.

Witch played restlessly with her hair, hiding her eyes with the brim of her hat as she looked at him. "Another…identification…perhaps?"

"Yes." Goblin Slayer nodded. Then, after a moment's thought, he added, "Will you do it?"

"…Let's, see." A beautiful hand was already reaching out. *Show me*, it seemed to say.

Goblin Slayer took the scroll he had just received out of his bag and handed it to her.

"I suppose…this is, from her…?"

"It is."

"Mm…" Witch nodded again, then turned the scroll in her palm a few times, after which she let out an impressed but still somehow lazy breath. "…That, woman. She's strange…is she, not?"

Goblin Slayer didn't answer. He didn't know people well enough to say. Didn't know *her* well enough.

So after another moment of thought, he said simply, "Is that so?" Witch nodded.

"Very…very…strange."

She set the scroll on the tabletop and produced a long pipe from the folds of her robe. She struck a flint with an elegant motion of her hands, lighting the pipe.

"Those who can become…like her. They number very, few. Outside…the logic, of the world. It's, very…scary there." A cloying aroma drifted around her. "Because you never know... And, anyone who can, go...to see her...is impressive, indeed."

Predictably, none of this made any sense to Goblin Slayer. "So what kind of scroll is it?"

"Heh, heh... This, see?" She gave the scroll a tap with the very tip of her finger. "It's a Gate...scroll."

"......Hmm."

"A mulligan. That's quite...a lucky find."

This was a magic item in the truest sense: a version of the lost Gate spell that anyone could use. It didn't matter if you were in the Dark Gods' tower, or some great wizard's underground labyrinth; you could escape in an instant. Just this scroll by itself could save your life. You could live to fight another day. The opportunity was worth thousands in gold. And even more so for a novice adventurer—use it or sell it, either way, the scroll was like a dream come true.

"...Is that so?"

Goblin Slayer didn't seem to fully comprehend it. Witch whispered, "That's right," then continued to weave her words together. "Write, a destination...and you can go, anywhere... Anywhere, in this world...at least."

But it had to be used thoughtfully. A chuckle escaped Witch.

"If you...tried to go to some, ruins at the bottom...of the sea? It would go there...and the water would drown you or wash you away."

Or, for example, you might jump through the Gate and be crushed to death...

This sort of conundrum was hardly unique to Gates. Anytime one used magic without thinking, it was tantamount to flirting with death. That was the real reason why it was said people without enough Intelligence couldn't become wizards. The job demanded study and care. What cards you had to play, when you should play them, what would happen: one had to think about all these things, make predictions, and try to achieve a certain outcome.

There was an extreme view that claimed there was no truth at all in the Ivory Tower, the academy of the sages. Knowledge and experience were the two main ingredients of Intelligence. Neither could be missing for anyone possessing true brains. Thus, it only made sense that novice wizards would go out into the world seeking real experience.

They had to know. Everything. All of it. And so they went into places unknown. That was praiseworthy, not something to be mocked. At least in principle.

Goblin Slayer thought Witch might be one of these spell casters errant. But he didn't know. He was not the kind to be interested in much of anyone's life history.

"...So. What...will you do with it?"

"What will I do with it?" He hadn't expected the question, and all he could do was parrot it back.

"The destination... You must write one, to be...able to use it, yes?" Witch's eyes wavered. Her actual expression, though, was hidden under her hat.

"A destination..."

"Yes." Witch puffed on her pipe, breathing out an aromatic haze that drifted around her. Then she spoke, her voice melodic, her words floating like the smoke through the air. "Someplace that is not here. Sometime that is not now. A last resort. A door for the going—or at, least, a simulacrum of one."

Her words seemed to dance through space, disappearing along with the smoke.

"That's, why...you must, write...a destination... See?"

"..." Goblin Slayer grunted softly. "I don't know."

"Mm..." Witch blinked, her long eyebrows fluttering. "Will you, sell it...?"

"I don't know that, either," Goblin Slayer said shortly, with a curt shake of his head.

"Think about it and decide." Witch passed the scroll back to him politely. Goblin Slayer grasped it in his hand.

"I don't have the ability to write a spell on a scroll."

Perhaps he meant, *Keep it for me.*

Witch thought about it for a moment, then took the scroll back and stashed it amid her ample cleavage.

"Can I ask you to take on this request?"

"It will, take some, time. Maybe...just, some?"

"I see."

"And now, I have…a date."

"I see," Goblin Slayer repeated, and then nodded. Then he counted out several gold pieces, payment in advance, and left the tavern behind.

§

"You," said Guild Girl, an unnatural smile pasted on her face, "are considered an outstanding adventurer."

"Really?!"

"Yes, everyone says you have big prospects for the future…"

"Well, now! Awesome…! I sure appreciate bein' appreciated!"

"On that basis, there's someone who says they would very much like to form a party with you."

"Yeah? Who is it that wants to party up with the great and mighty—I mean, who wants to join my party?"

"A highly intelligent wizard who's seen exactly how powerful you are. You remember the temporary party…"

"Ahh, that witch…!" The adventurer, lightly armored and carrying a spear on his back, recalled her immediately.

Guild Girl was privately relieved. Her cheek was twitching. She couldn't let the smile down yet.

"What did you think of her? She was a good adventurer, wasn't she?"

"Yeah, great!" Spearman said, puffing out his chest. "She seemed like a pretty capable spell caster to me!"

Guild Girl didn't honestly know whether that was true or not. She had never seen an actual adventure with her own eyes. Her fights and adventures took place with a pen and paper.

And negotiations.

She worked hard to pull up her cheeks, which continued to twitch as she said, "What do you say, then? Would you be open to partying up with her again?"

"You can count on me! Heck, if I had a spell caster, I would be like a tiger with wings! I won't let anyone down!" Spearman gave a broad grin and nodded vigorously, apparently happy to have been entrusted with this request.

He didn't see the shadow of calculation. Guild Girl, for her part, said, "Thank you very much for handling this," and bowed her head. She felt a little bad for him.

"Okay!" Spearman exclaimed. He gave one bow, then rushed off in a fit of excitement.

"Oh, I think she's at the tavern!" Guild Girl called after him. Then she let out a sort of "Oof" noise and slid down onto the counter.

She hadn't lied to him. Everything she'd said had been true.

Spearman did indeed have a favorable reputation. And there was no question that he was capable. That Witch wanted to work with him was a fact, too. Facts all.

She found herself rubbing at her own cheeks. Having to pretend to smile all the time was so tiring. Spearman was one thing, but there were so many flippant young adventurers who were all talk. They focused on raising people's impressions of them, while avoiding responsibility and real work, always looking for the easiest ways to turn a profit.

Everyone had that side to them; she couldn't condemn them for it. They were free to think that was good and fine, but...

I'm free not to like them very much for it, too.

At least that spear-wielding adventurer had a few achievements to his name. If he hadn't, she would never have gone to this sort of trouble for him.

"Tired?"

"Yeah..."

Her colleague smiled sympathetically from the next chair.

"Well, adventuring attracts all types. Try not to worry too much about it, okay?"

"I know that... I do."

In the end, work is work, her colleague reminded her. Wonderful adventurers, despicable adventurers—they would all die someday. The gods' dice treated all fairly and equally; thus, individual effort or lack thereof could affect the possibilities.

All the more reason it was better not to be involved with anyone except when called upon.

We are not in an especially exalted position...

That was one of the first things she'd been taught when she became a member of the staff of the Adventurers Guild. Guild Girl did understand that.

Or at least, I feel like I do, but...

"...I'm going to go put some tea on."

"Great! Make some for me too, okay?"

"Yeah, sure," she said to her pestering colleague as she stood up.

She placed a sign that said BE BACK SOON at her counter and retreated to a back room.

She could and should boil the water herself, but...

Nothing wrong with a little laziness.

Guild Girl poked her head into the kitchen and asked for some boiling water. The rhea chef there was easygoing.

She waited until the tea leaves had steeped, poured some in her favorite cup, then bustled back to the reception counter.

"Here you go."

"Yay! Thank you!" Her coworker happily took the cup; Guild Girl ignored her when she asked, "How about some snacks to go with?"

Guild Girl sat in her own seat and was just putting her cup to her lips, when—

"Oh!"

She put the cup back down on the saucer with a clatter.

A dark figure was striding boldly through the crowded Guild Hall. He wore grimy leather armor and a cheap-looking steel helmet. A sword of a strange length was at his hip, and a small round shield was on his arm.

It was the adventurer they had come to call...

...Goblin Slayer.

As he walked toward her, Guild Girl put her hands neatly in her lap, blushing when her coworker noticed her.

"Er, uh," she said, sitting up straighter. "Wh-what can I do for you today?"

"Goblins."

One sure word. The same one every time. Guild Girl felt her cheeks pull toward a frown, although for a different reason from earlier.

"But…you just handled some goblins recently, right?"

I'm sure… She didn't even have to check the paperwork. He hardly, if ever, took quests other than goblin hunting.

Otherwise, they wouldn't have called him Goblin Slayer.

"Maybe you'd like to take on something else for a change? Like, uh, a Manticore or something…?!"

"No." He shook his head. "Goblins."

Hmm… Guild Girl pursed her lips worriedly. She felt like all those trips to that wizard's place recently had changed him somewhat, but…

At last, she gave a long, resigned sigh and said, "All right." Then a nod. "I'll have a look… Oh, have some tea, if you like."

"Yes."

Thankfully, she hadn't taken a sip from the cup yet. She offered the tea to him and started flipping through pages. There was no end to goblin-hunting quests in the world. There was a half-joking proverb that held "every time a party of new adventurers is formed, so is a goblin nest." That's how ubiquitous they were.

"Uh, here. There's…two today. These ones."

"I'll take them both," he declared without even looking at the quest papers, causing Guild Girl to smile awkwardly again. If an adventurer was willing to take on goblin quests, though, she wasn't going to turn him down. The main thing was that he got the job done—like that spearman.

"I'm going, then."

"Uh, right! Be careful!"

Goblin Slayer did the absolute minimum of paperwork, then walked away as boldly as he had come.

"Not the warmest guy around, is he?" Guild Girl's colleague smirked as he left.

"No…" Guild Girl agreed.

He didn't chat. He attended only to what was necessary. And then he did what he had to do. And…

The cup… It's…empty?

She didn't know how he drank through his visor, but somehow the fact made her very happy.

"…Heh-heh!"

Guild Girl pursued her work cheerfully all afternoon and well into the evening.

§

"GOROOGORO!!"

He stopped the screaming, onrushing goblin with his shield and a slight "Hmph," and the creature bounced back. Jumping ability didn't vary much from one goblin to the next. Not even if the creature was clinging to a tree root poking down through the ceiling of the cave.

So it was possible to learn and be prepared for them.

Goblin Slayer moved in on the downed monster and stabbed him in the throat.

"GOBGRG?!"

"Three," he said as he looked down at the expiring monster, choking on a geyser of its own blood.

Very few goblin-slaying quests are truly unique.

This one simply involved a goblin nest that had appeared near a farming village, nothing special. He'd visited Arc Mage, then dropped by the Guild, prepared some food, and set out. A few perfunctory greetings at the village, then directly to the cave.

Goblin Slayer had entered the cave at twilight, prepared for the little devils to resist him. Night belonged to the Non-Prayer Characters.

"…Hrm."

Now though, as he kicked the goblin corpse over into a corner, Goblin Slayer grumbled to himself. There weren't nearly as many guards here as he had expected.

Aren't goblins active at night?

Their eyes could see in the dark, letting them traverse the shadows to attack a village, looking to steal livestock or crops or women.

That was how goblins worked. Even children knew it. And yet…

"…"

Was that why?

The possibility came to him in a flash, like intuition, like inspiration, but he shook his head and said, "No, it can't be."

He couldn't jump to any conclusions based on guesswork. Observe, confirm. Consider soberly. Wasn't that what he had been taught?

He pulled his sword out of the goblin's throat, wiping it on the creature's loincloth. Then he dropped into a low stance, proceeding one careful step at a time.

There was some filth here, but there were no bugs, no bat excrement—probably, he thought, because they had all been turned into meals already.

The cave was not all that large. Before his first torch had burned down, he'd found the room he was looking for.

"I thought so."

The words escaped him without his really meaning them to. His intuition had been correct.

They're sleeping.

It was, in practical terms, a goblin sleeping chamber. Here, deep in the cave, five or six goblins lay abed.

It must be "dawn" for them right now.

The goblins had learned at some point that adventurers came during the day. Thus, it made perfect sense for them to post guards in the middle of their night—people did the same thing. The night watch was an important duty.

But "early morning"… Perhaps that was different.

No such thing as a hard-working goblin, eh?

Even the handful of guards had looked sleepy. The goblins who had foisted the duty on them were in dreamland.

No goblin, it seemed, would purposely get up early to perform a trying task for the sake of his comrades.

If one were not among those who had words… If one were a goblin…

A face flashed through his mind. That girl. Was she waiting for him today, too? At the farm. Until morning.

Goblin Slayer set the torch delicately on the ground, grabbed his sword in a reverse grip, then walked carefully into the room.

He put his hand over the mouth of the nearest goblin, simultaneously stabbing him in the throat and slashing.

"GBBG?!"

The monster's eyes flew open and he opened his mouth to shout, but only a few garbled syllables came out. And those were muffled by the hand, and then the monster slumped down, dead.

"...Four."

Soundless, unnoticed, Goblin Slayer went about his business quickly and quietly so that none of the creatures would wake up. He hardly breathed; he stepped as silently as he could, performing his task with an almost benevolent detachment.

It was an exhausting way to do things. All the more reason he needed to remain detached, treat it like business. Pay attention to what warranted attention and ignore everything else. That way he could stave off the fatigue.

"Five... Hrm?"

Goblin Slayer executed another goblin. But the feel was wrong; he clicked his tongue when he saw the blade of his sword was dulled with blood and fat. He was about to throw the weapon away—

"GOBBGR..."

—when suddenly there came a mumbling from one corner of the room, and Goblin Slayer immediately flung his sword in that direction.

It sliced through the darkness, landing in a goblin's throat with a dull thump, taking his life. The creature crumpled back and died, never knowing what was a dream and what was reality.

The sound of the corpse collapsing to the ground made Goblin Slayer nervous; he grabbed a club lying at his feet. He ducked down low, watching the surviving goblins closely as the last of the echoes faded.

"GOBGR?!" One of them spoke. He swung out with his right arm. Muttering and mumbling, the goblin turned over in his sleep.

Goblin Slayer slowly let out a breath.

Three left.

It would be a certain amount of trouble, but it never even occurred to him to resent it. If he could have washed them all away with a flood, it might have been slightly more efficient, but...

"...Hmph."

It was worth thinking about. Goblin Slayer nodded, then walked toward the remaining goblins.

By midnight, it was all over.

§

"Ahh, man, now I'm running late…!"

It wasn't that far from the farm to the town, but after factoring in the time it took to get ready, and sometimes hurrying became a necessity. Considering the amount of cargo, she didn't really need a horse, and in the end, Cow Girl pulled the cart herself, huffing and puffing.

'Fraid this is gonna make me all muscly.

That wasn't necessarily a bad thing, and it would have happened naturally in the course of doing farmwork. But be that as it may, as a young girl, she wasn't sure she fancied the idea…

No sooner had the thought crossed her mind than she giggled, finding it strange that she should have considered such a thing at all.

I never used to be even slightly worried about that sort of thing.

She wiped the sweat trickling down her brow, breathing deeply as she pulled the cart around behind the Guild building.

This was hardly the end of it; she still had to unload the cargo.

There were stories in the world of a carpet that would produce food just by unfurling it, or a spoon from which soup bubbled up endlessly. But the Adventurers Guild tavern possessed nothing of the sort; they used fresh ingredients every day.

With an encouraging *hup*, she got started: grab a box or a barrel, set it down, grab another one, set it down. There were a great many boxes and barrels to pick up and move since eating and drinking were among the chief pleasures of the town's adventurers.

After everything was unloaded and the paperwork was done, the sweat wasn't just trickling; she was soaked in it.

Cow Girl sat down on a nearby barrel, leaning against a wall in exhaustion.

"Pheeew… *Now* I'm tired…"

She opened the collar of her sopping shirt, which stuck to her skin, fanning her chest to get a breeze going. She looked at the sky and saw that twilight was near; the cool breeze on her flushed cheeks felt lovely.

Next, she cast her gaze to the side and saw some adventurers. Were they heading out, or coming home? They went in and out of the Guild, wearing and carrying every conceivable type of equipment.

She watched intently, searching the crowd for a cheap-looking steel helmet with horns.

Not here, huh? Didn't think so.

She had expected as much. Or did she just want to think that? Lately, he'd started coming home only near dawn. Today, once again, he'd left early in the morning, and she didn't expect him back tonight.

Anyway, if she *had* seen him there at twilight, it would have only made her wonder what he was doing with all those hours until he came home in the morning. *Sure.*

"...Ergh."

An image of him and some woman, like hazy graffiti, drifted through her mind, and she felt a flush rise to her cheeks.

This is all because Uncle said those nasty things...

She hadn't been aware of it, but it seemed his words still lingered in her mind.

Yes, she understood that men were like that, sort of, but still...

Cow Girl shook her head vigorously, trying to drive away the ugly imaginings.

"Hey, have you heard?"

"About what?"

"Goblin Slayer."

Just who she'd been thinking of—she perked up her ears.

Breathing as quietly as she could and paying careful attention to her footsteps, she climbed down off the barrel and slid closer along the wall.

A couple of adventurers were chatting outside the door of the Guild Hall. One of them appeared to be a young warrior, but as for the other, Cow Girl couldn't guess at his profession. He wore leather armor, and a sword hung at his hip. So did a helmet, but that was about all she could see. She didn't know if he was a warrior or a scout, or some sort of blend of the two classes.

These are real adventurers, she realized, her eyes going wide, and kept herself hidden against the wall without really knowing why.

"Who's that again?"

"You know, the guy who only ever hunts goblins."

"Err.........?"

"He registered the same day I did... Oh, and he never takes his helmet off."

"Ahh, yeah, the sorta filthy one."

Cow Girl had something to say about that, but she had nothing even resembling the courage to jump out and confront the men. She took slow, deep breaths, trying to soothe the nameless anxiety that made her heart pound in her chest.

He was called Goblin Slayer. She knew that. It was all right. She already knew.

"Okay, so, this Goblin Killer or whatever. What about him?"

"Goblin *Slayer*," the young warrior corrected the other adventurer with a frown. "Anyway, I hear he's been going to that shack on the riverside."

"The riverside...," the other adventurer said, and then, after some thought, he said, "You mean where that freaky lady lives?"

Lady.

Cow Girl swallowed hard. She grabbed the loosened collar of her shirt.

No, it was too soon. She couldn't draw any conclusions yet. She should wait. Yeah, wait.

"You know her?"

"She's this weird...sage or mage or something. Doin' some kind of 'research.'" The hostility was plain in the adventurer's voice; perhaps he had some sort of unpleasant memories of this woman. "I went to her for an identification once, and she was all, 'Surely you don't need me to identify something *this* obvious.'"

"She chased you out?"

"Out? I never even got in the front door."

"Let me guess—it turned out to be junk anyway."

"I took it to her because nothing happened when I used it... Eh, turned out to be that sort of staff."

"A magic staff, huh? So what was the effect?"

"When y'hold it, you won't fall down."

The adventurers shared a dry laugh. Had that been some sort of joke? You carried a staff exactly so that you wouldn't fall down when walking.

Cow Girl scraped at the flagstones with her toes, totally lost as to the meaning of the adventurers' conversation. She wasn't interested in their strange jokes. She wanted to know about the other thing they'd said. Before that.

"So, hey, why worry about this...uh..."

"Goblin Slayer."

"Yeah. Why worry about him anyway?"

"Well, we came in at the same time," the young warrior said softly, his expression difficult to read. "I thought maybe he'd joined a party or something, and I can't get the thought out of my head."

"You're solo yourself, ain'tcha? Wanna join up with someone? I could introduce you."

"No, I'm—" He shook his head slowly. "Fine like this, for now."

"Yeah, okay," the other adventurer answered, and then a smile with a hint of malice came over his face. "Too busy watching out for newbies, huh? Gotcher eye on that silver-haired gal?"

"No. No, not really," the young warrior said indignantly, but then he soon wore a relaxed smiled. "Anyway, never mind about me. So you're saying he's partied up with that spell caster?"

Yes, this was it. Cow Girl gulped, leaning out from the shadows ever so slightly.

"Dunno. Can't say she looked like the type."

For better or for worse, the adventurers were so caught up in their discussion that neither of them looked her way. Cow Girl listened with every iota of her being, like the adventurer who robbed the dragon's hoard in the story she'd heard growing up.

The adventurer who seemed to know something about the spell caster was trying to explain to the warrior, but he found the subject hard to articulate, and his explanation was hard to follow.

"She wears this dirty robe, and her room is full of all this junk. And it smells funny, like medicine or something."

"Huh… An alchemist, maybe?"

"Maybe. She sure don't look like an adventurer. If she were the studious, scholarly type, I'd have chatted her up already."

"C'mon, now…" *You've got a weird type.* The young warrior sighed, shaking his head slowly. "I guess Goblin Slayer doesn't seem like the type to party up, either…"

"Yeah, but they're both kinda dirty. Birds of a feather, y'know?"

Cow Girl found the sound escaping her: "Wha?!" One of the adventurers let out a puzzled "Hrm?" and she quickly clapped a hand over her mouth.

"What's up?"

"I thought— Eh, probably my imagination. Not like there're gonna be any monsters in town anyway."

"The heck are you talking about?"

I found this shop with a cute waitress. She's totally into me. What, this again? No, it's for real this time. Let's go.

Thus conversing, they faded into the evening crowd. Cow Girl stayed in the shadows, watching them leave. So he *was* frequenting a woman's house. They were doing something together. Apparently. Apparently?

Not that it was anything to be so shocked about… At least, that's what she thought. Probably, she was pretty sure.

The relationship between him and her was just that between the landlord's daughter—no, his niece—and a tenant. Nothing more and nothing less.

She still had secrets, things she hadn't told him.

And surely he, too, had things he hadn't told her.

She was getting too involved. Just butting in. So…

"Birds of a feather. Birds of a feather……"

She covered her face with her hands, feeling like she had no idea what to do. The odors of sweat and dust stung her eyes, tickled the inside of her nose. She rubbed her face with her palm.

"……I'm going home."

Yes, she would go home.

The sky was crimson already; night was near. The wind was cold, and her body felt so heavy.

Going home would be the best thing.

Even if she knew he wouldn't be there that night.

§

The Adventurers Guild was already cloaked in silence by the time he got there.

The lamplight was kept to a minimum to conserve fuel, casting the hall in a clinging dimness.

At the reception desk, the night staff member—Guild Girl—sat in her chair, her head bobbing as she dreamed.

Despite the smells of rust and mud that accompanied him, Goblin Slayer walked without making a sound. With the quill pen that sat ready on the reception desk, he wrote a simple report on some sheep-skin paper, set it down gently, then put a paperweight on top of it.

"...? Oh... Er, oh...!"

At that moment, Guild Girl came to with a small squeak, shivering as she looked up. When she first took in the steel helmet, she flinched backward, but then hurriedly straightened up so she was sitting properly.

"I-I'm sorry. That was very rude of me. Um..."

"My report," Goblin Slayer said. Then, as if it had just occurred to him, he added, "From the goblin hunt."

"Uh, right..." Guild Girl took the paper in hand and skimmed it. Sitting up even straighter, she said, "I'll have a look at it."

A scrawl of writing ran across the paper, as if it had been thrown onto the page. He himself felt it was abominable penmanship. His older sister had taught him to read and write back when he was very young. He'd had few chances to use the skill since then.

Even if your letters aren't very nice, if you write carefully, it'll be okay.

So his sister had told him. He thought he had tried to write carefully.

"Okay, good... Um, was there anything unusual?"

"There were goblins," he said. "Not very many. I killed them all."

"...Sounds like everything's in order, then."

Guild Girl giggled quietly, double-checked the paperwork politely, and nodded. She put the report carefully into a paper holder and filed it away.

"I deem this quest finished. Good work! I'll get your reward ready now."

"…"

Guild Girl lifted her bottom out of the chair to stand. Goblin Slayer's helmet turned in the direction of the workshop. The lights were all out, as expected. The fires of the forge were probably still burning, but even if he requested something from them now, they probably wouldn't start working on it until the next day.

"…No," he said, shaking his head. "I will take it tomorrow."

"Are you sure?"

The helmet moved again, nodding this time. He seemed to think this marked the end of the conversation.

Uh, well, then. Guild Girl, however, moved her fingers restlessly, as if there was still something more she wanted to say.

Goblin Slayer waited silently. "Ahemmm," she managed. "As a matter of fact, this quest was issued a number of days ago, but nobody would take it…"

"Is that so?"

"Well, the reward isn't very good. But, uhh…"

"What?"

She sucked in a breath, causing her ample chest to rise, and the rest of her words came out in a stream. "So you've really been a big help! Thank you very much!"

Goblin Slayer merely replied, "I see."

Then, with one of his characteristically blunt "All rights", he headed directly for the door, leaving a trail of muddy footprints.

He pushed the double doors open and went outside, listening to them fall silent behind him as he looked up at the sky. The light of the stars was faint, and the moons were shadowed as well. A pale light was already visible at the edges of the eastern sky.

"Hrm," he breathed quietly, and then he walked down the path with his bold, indifferent stride.

It would soon be summer, but the morning air was still cold. He could feel the dew as he walked.

The farmhouse wasn't far, and his feet knew the way well, but sometimes it seemed to take a surprisingly long time. Maybe he was tired. That was his conclusion, feeling as if he were watching himself from behind.

And then he didn't think any further about it. There were other things that required his attention, his consideration. The underbrush nearby, the shadows of trees, the far side of the spreading field. Was there nothing moving there? And if there was, what was it? Any footprints? Any tracks? He didn't sense any aura of anything, that ill-defined presence.

"*Aura?*" his master had demanded. "*Who believes in that sort of crap?*"

Everything could be understood by seeing, hearing, smelling, touching, tasting.

"*Then you've just got to think about what it* means."

That was what his master had smirkingly declared after the usual round of battering him.

"*There're those who can get to a conclusion without thinking, but you, you're too stupid for that, understand? ...Take it as a rule of thumb.*"

Then his master had kicked him back down again as he tried to get up, and he had gone tumbling across the ice.

It was then that he had learned his teacher was apt to do such things. But only later would he come to understand that knowing something and being able to act on it were different things.

"......"

When he got to the farm, he noticed himself immediately making a circuit of the fence.

That was a bad sign.

Checking for the enemy should be a habit, but it shouldn't become habitual, shouldn't be performed by rote. That would give the goblins the chance to sneak by him. It would leave him unable to respond to a goblin who did something different from usual.

He shook his head to free his helmet from the dew, went back the way he'd come, and started again. When he'd finished a complete circuit, there was still time before sunrise. He went to his shed and took out some daggers and broken helmets, placing them on a shelf.

It must have been the fatigue that made his arms and legs feel heavy. But there were no guarantees that goblins wouldn't appear when he was tired.

"…Hrm."

He grasped a dagger in shaking fingers, took up a stance, and flung it. Miss. Another throw. Hit.

That wasn't good enough. He didn't want to know that he *had* hit but to be sure that he *would* hit.

When he ran out of knives, he collected the daggers from his missed throws and tried again, until all the helmets had been knocked down.

It was about then that the sun was finally peeking over the horizon. He squinted behind his visor against a light that seemed to stab through his eyes and into his brain.

"…Hrm." He grunted briefly. In the new light, he could see that parts of the stone wall were broken down.

Goblins?

That wasn't the only explanation. It could be some child's prank. Or perhaps it had just crumbled naturally. There was nothing that didn't need upkeep. He collected the helmets and daggers and set them aside, then walked over to the wall. He crouched down, running a hand along it carefully to check it. He decided that no person (or, by extension, goblin) had done this. He let out a breath.

"…You're quite the hard worker."

That was when he heard a voice behind him, unexpected. He stood slowly.

It was the owner of the farm, probably come out of the main house. He looked like he had just gotten up, but he was fully awake.

"One man alone just can't do everything, you see? It would mean a lot to me if you'd help."

The owner stood with the sun at his back, watching Goblin Slayer, who replied, "More to the point," and shook his head softly. "It would mean trouble if goblins came here."

"…" The owner made some kind of face, but he appeared as a shadow to Goblin Slayer, who couldn't make out his expression. Then the owner crossed his arms and made a sound somewhat like a cow makes, deep in its throat. "…About the girl…"

Goblin Slayer straightened up. "Yes, sir."

"She came home awfully depressed last night."

"…"

"Try to…have some consideration for her, maybe."

Goblin Slayer was silent, his helmet fixed in the direction of the owner, who started to shift uncomfortably.

"Have consideration," Goblin Slayer echoed. "Meaning?"

"I mean… Pay her some mind, spend some time with her… It could mean a lot of things."

It was a terribly vague response; the owner himself sounded like he wasn't quite sure of the answer. But Goblin Slayer replied, "I see," and nodded. It sounded, to an extent, like something he could do. "I will try."

"…Right. I hope you will." The farm owner let out a breath, visibly relieved, then turned around and headed back into the main house. Halfway there, though, he stopped. "And also," he added over his shoulder. "Clean yourself up a little… You smell something awful."

Goblin Slayer thought for a moment but ultimately said nothing as he watched the owner go. The odor was, after all, a necessity for killing goblins.

"……"

Still holding the helmets and daggers, Goblin Slayer went back in the shed, tossing them in a corner. In their place, he took out the oil-soaked rag he used to prepare his equipment. Still silent, he ran it over every surface of his armor. Even then, it could hardly have been called clean. But he threw the rag aside when he was done wiping and headed directly for the house.

There came a sudden creaking ache in his head, which he decided must be due to dehydration. He would need to have water before he slept for an hour or two.

"…Oh, welcome home."

No sooner had he opened the door than a rich and familiar aroma greeted him. *She* was standing there in the kitchen with her apron on, smiling hesitantly in front of a pot over the fire.

"Er, uh… Want some breakfast?"

Goblin Slayer thought for just a moment before responding, "I will have some."

"Oh, ah, r-right…!"

She turned into a flurry of activity around the kitchen, setting out dishes. He glanced in the direction of the table, where the farm owner, already seated, was shooting him a hard look.

Goblin Slayer sat down across from him, uncertain of what to say. But before long, he offered softly, "Tomorrow, I believe I will be able to pay rent again."

"…That right?"

A few moments later, breakfast was on the table in front of him. It was stew.

Words of thanks were said, and breakfast began. Goblin Slayer moved his spoon silently.

"…"

"…"

Cow Girl was looking at him as if she wanted to say something.

Goblin Slayer considered but, unable to think of anything, stayed quiet.

At last, she closed her mouth again, dropping her eyes to her place setting.

So Goblin Slayer put his spoon in his empty bowl and said, "…What should I do?"

"Huh?"

"…"

"…Er…" She couldn't quite get anything out; she looked to her uncle, flummoxed, for help. He shrugged silently. "…I'm…going to make some deliveries," she said.

"I see."

"You're…saying you'll help me…?"

That…makes me happy, I think. At that, Goblin Slayer repeated, "I see." Then: "Wait an hour."

"Oh, uh, sure!" Cow Girl nodded so hard her whole body shook. "Okay. I'll be waiting!"

Goblin Slayer stood without another word and left the house at a stride. Maybe it was the flavor of the food, or the fatigue that dogged him, but his legs felt as heavy as if he were manacled.

Still, he brought each foot up, then set it down, working his way forward. As long as he kept going forward, he would reach his destination. Eventually. He would get there.

He entered the shed, sat down against the wall, and closed his eyes.

It's all the same, Goblin Slayer thought.

All things should be habit, but not habitual, not performed by rote.

All things should be studied, then considered, and then acted upon.

But he also knew that studying something didn't translate into the ability to put it into practice.

Sometimes things simply didn't go the way you planned.

§

Cow Girl peeked into the shed, uncertain what to do. She could see him sitting curled down in a corner of the characteristically cluttered building.

Not sitting… He's asleep.

He had come home from work, eaten enough to fill his stomach, then sat down and slept. To think that he would then help her with her own chores while barely pausing for some rest honestly didn't make her happy.

On the other hand, she wanted to do something with him—something that didn't involve goblins.

No. Stop pretending.

She was genuinely pleased that he had eaten the meal she'd made and had said he would help her. That was the emotion foremost in her mind, for better or for worse.

So that's…why I nodded.

"……Sigh."

Unable to make a decision, Cow Girl looked back and forth between the cart, all ready to go, and the pale darkness.

An hour had passed already. They had some leeway, sure, but this was fresh produce. It couldn't sit forever.

She had been standing indecisively for several minutes when she heard the distant lowing of a cow, and she let out a breath.

She gave a gentle tap on the already open door and called to him, "…Hey, you awake?"

"…" He rose heavily, not saying a word. Cow Girl squeaked without meaning to.

"Y-you were already awake…?"

Then he'd seen her standing there fidgeting and thinking.

Her voice had started to scratch, but he replied, "No," as curt as ever. "I just woke up." He sounded a touch hoarse. "I'm sorry."

"N-no problem…" Cow Girl shook her head gently. "It's okay… I'm fine."

"I see."

He took a long swig from a carafe of water (when had he gotten that?), and then, after a moment's silence, he started walking. His stride was bold and without hesitation; he passed by Cow Girl quickly.

"Oh wait…!" He was already picking up the crossbar of the cart and preparing to head out by the time she called after him.

"What?" He paused respectfully.

Cow Girl fretted about what to say, but finally decided to simply say what she was thinking. "I-I'll go with you, so…!"

"I see."

Cow Girl jogged over and fell in behind the cart. His visor might have hidden his face, but she still didn't have the courage to walk alongside him.

"O-okay, here we go!"

"Yes." The response was as brief and detached as ever. Cow Girl gave the cart her mightiest shove, thinking that maybe this was the best she could hope for.

The wheels started turning with a creak, then settled lazily into motion.

It all seemed so much easier than usual. Maybe it was because he was pulling for her.

"It's n-not too heavy…?"

"No."

Hardly any words at all. She thought about how tired he must be, but she didn't say anything.

"…"

"…"

They walked together under the morning sky, in time with the wheels' creaking and the summer wind gusting past them. When Cow Girl looked straight ahead, all she could see was a pile of produce; she had to peek around the side to catch a glimpse of him. Even then, of course, she could only see his back and his steel helmet.

"Uh, it's getting warmer, huh?"

"Is that so?"

"It might get hot... Summer's coming and all."

"Yes."

"Aren't you warm?"

"No."

Cow Girl fell quiet. Neither of them spoke further. She settled back in behind the cart, looking at her feet and focusing on pushing. Sweat ran down her forehead and dribbled onto the ground.

It was a short trip from the farm to town, a small blessing—perhaps. She didn't have much hope that she would be able to hold any kind of long conversation with him.

More than anything, though, she didn't want him to see her like this.

Even she knew how unhappy she must have looked.

§

They passed through the gate into town, and when they had pulled up in front of the Guild, he stopped the cart. Cow Girl only noticed when the creaking of the wheels ceased. She hurriedly let go of the cart, and meanwhile, he came up beside her with his casual gait.

"I'll unload."

"Oh, r-right."

His tone brooked no argument. Cow Girl nodded and reached out for the pile of produce herself.

She caught a sidelong look at him as he silently hefted up the heavy wooden boxes and set them down.

As for Cow Girl, she couldn't do it—even though she was finally here, huffing and puffing and working away.

I guess it must be...because he's an adventurer.

She couldn't tell under all that armor, but she assumed he must be pretty well built.

"What's wrong?"

"N-nothing…!"

She realized she'd been staring at him so intently that she had stopped moving, and she quickly went back to work. She still didn't know what to talk about, but at least this time, she knew what she ought to do.

It was good to have work to do, Cow Girl thought. Pick up the cargo, set it down, pick up some more. Again and again.

Even once they had finished that job, next they had to hand it over to the Guild. Cow Girl wiped the sweat from her brow and steadied her breathing as she looked at him.

"……"

"So, um…"

She couldn't quite speak. It wasn't because of the harshness of her breath. The cat had her tongue.

She kicked listlessly at the flagstones with her toes. He watched her silently.

It was intensely uncomfortable, and Cow Girl looked at the ground. "It's… Yeah. It's okay now. Thanks."

"I see."

Is that it?

But naturally, she still couldn't bring herself to voice the question.

He nodded curtly, then turned around and began striding away. She could only stand there and watch him go. She reached out her hand, then drew it back, clutched it to her chest.

She felt so warm. Maybe it was the sweat. The warmth burned in her chest. Maybe it was because of her hand? Maybe both.

"……"

Cow Girl stood that way for a while, looking up at the sky. It was painfully blue.

…This has to stop.

She shook her head, feeling, somehow, completely pathetic.

She knocked on the back door of the Guild and let the staff know their order was here. She got the signature on her paper.

They told her a few other minor details had to be taken care of, and she frowned, having forgotten this part. It meant she would have to go into the Guild lobby. Where he was.

"Something the matter?"

"Oh no." The staff member appeared worried about her, but Cow Girl simply shook her head. "It's just hot today."

"Ahh. It's almost summer, isn't it?"

Trivial chitchat. The sort of banal exchange she simply couldn't have with him.

Cow Girl felt it squeezing her heart as she said, "Okay, then," and quickly excused herself.

She pattered along, feeling like she was swimming in a sea of lively adventurers, toward the Guild Hall.

It overwhelmed her no matter how many times she saw it—almost made her dizzy.

There were so many people there, wearing every kind of gear, carrying every type of item imaginable. She scanned the panoply of equipment for someone trudging his way along in grimy leather armor and a helmet.

"Oh…"

There he was—sitting on a bench in a corner of the waiting room. Cow Girl found she couldn't speak to him immediately.

"___"

"_____"

She didn't know what he was doing. But beside him was the figure of a woman.

She was beautiful. Her clothing clearly traced along the alluring lines of her body, her face hidden under a broad-brimmed hat.

That was the adventurer Cow Girl had engaged for a brief job once. Now she was talking with him, in what seemed to be a very chipper mood. She laughed as she passed him some kind of scroll.

"…"

Cow Girl could feel the heat drain from her chest, and she shook her head, dazed.

That can't… That can't be her.

It couldn't be. The rumors had been about someone in robes, a strange woman who gave off the same vibes as he did.

Not her—probably not, Cow Girl thought.

"Oh…"

He was looking her way.

He had only moved his helmet, but somehow, she knew.

They must have been done talking. He nodded briefly to the witch, then strode over in Cow Girl's direction.

"Wha— Ah— Oh…"

Cow Girl was nearly frantic. She'd never imagined he would come up to her.

Maybe he wouldn't realize she'd seen him. But what if he did?

Well, what if he did? It wasn't like she'd done anything wrong. But still…

"What's wrong?"

"N-nothing's, er, wrong." Her voice went up an octave and the end of her sentence jumped. It was a pretty poor job of lying, if she said so herself.

But he only breathed, "I see," and nodded that helmeted head.

Did—did he believe me?

He didn't speak, yet, she was terrified. He was often silent and said little even when he did talk. So this was perfectly normal, and yet…

What was he like, when we were little?

She felt like she remembered him talking quite a bit. But that had been five years ago. As clear as the memory felt, she found the details hazy.

What about him? she wondered. How much did he remember of her from five years before?

Cow Girl had no way of knowing.

"Is there something else you need help with?"

"N-no… It's all right. I'm fine."

"I see."

And there, of course, the conversation ended.

Cow Girl looked from the floor to the helmet and back, then noticed that passing adventurers were staring at them.

Maybe they were standing too close to the entrance. The adventurers went by, casting sidelong glances their way.

I could maybe blend in, but I guess he stands out...

Cow Girl smiled ruefully to herself. She reached out toward his sleeve, but in the end, she let her hand drop.

"Let's move over to the side, okay?"

"Yes."

It wouldn't do to be in the way. She moved aside a few steps, and a second later, he followed her.

...I feel like he's...taller than before, maybe.

She'd never had to raise her eyes to look him in the face in the past.

She'd always believed she could beat him in a fight. Or a footrace, or anything.

Not anymore.

The feeling became a sigh that slipped out of her mouth.

Predictably, he tilted his steel helmet and asked, "What's wrong?" but she once again repeated, "Nothing."

There was nothing in the world that didn't change.

In the course of five years, everything changed.

I wonder if I was...a nuisance.

He didn't say anything. Of course not. And Cow Girl didn't have the courage to ask. The chattering of adventurers all around her had grown so grating. She couldn't stand it.

She opened her mouth, even though she wasn't sure what she was going to do with it. "H-hey, um..."

"You're *here*!!"

At that instant, a voice that sounded like the ringing of a bell cut through the noise of the crowd. Cow Girl looked up in surprise and turned to see a small figure hurrying toward them.

The rush of the air blew back the person's hood, revealing an intelligent face, eyes gleaming—a woman.

She was coming at them like a cat pouncing on its prey...

"Oh..."

"You didn't come by today, so I'd given up on seeing you. Gosh, and there I was, waiting for you the whole time!"

An instant later, the woman had passed Cow Girl by and swept *him* up in a great hug.

He ignored Cow Girl's astonished stare, saying only, "I see," and nodding.

"But I, in my magnanimity, shall forgive you! Considering that your diligence takes so much of the work out of finding you."

"Is that so?"

"It is indeed!"

The woman—even Cow Girl could tell she was a wizard—continued to embrace him with unfettered joy, chattering away. Oddly, though, the overall murmur of the room didn't seem to encompass this spell caster. Only he and Cow Girl had noticed her. Cow Girl blinked, feeling as if her world were being torn apart.

"My hopes and dreams are about to be realized, but there's a problem! I desperately want your help, what do you think?"

"Goblins?"

"Unfortunately, most sadly, and very happily, that is indeed the case!"

"I see," he said again, the helmet turning to look around.

Cow Girl shivered as the gaze behind the visor settled on her.

"I'm sorry, but I have a quest."

"Er, ah, a—q-quest?"

"Yes."

Cow Girl bit her lip, wringing her hands together.

She couldn't accept this. How could she ever accept this?

She couldn't accept this, but they were a quest giver and an adventurer, or so he said. And in that case…

"…Then my only choice is to understand."

"I see."

Still those same two words, still the end of the conversation. Cow Girl, unable to say anything else, dropped her eyes to her feet again.

That's why she didn't notice. Didn't see the wizard—Arc Mage—look from her to him and back and nod knowingly.

"Well, goodness gracious me. Right. You, go get provisions from the tavern."

"Mm." He grunted, but then repeated quietly, "Me?"

"Surely you don't mean to make a girl carry the cargo," Arc Mage said. She snapped her fingers as if she were performing a magic spell and took out a gold coin. "Cider, too, of course. Take *plenty* of time deciding what we need—consider that an order from your quest giver."

"...Me?"

"Yes, you."

Goblin Slayer grunted again, then said simply, "Understood," and took the coin.

Cow Girl's face was starting to crumple, like a child who had been left out of a game.

"Oh, heavens," Arc Mage said, and laughed uncomfortably. "Don't make that face. This isn't what you think it is."

"...Really?"

"I promise. Never has been, never will be." Arc Mage chuckled and brushed Cow Girl's face. Cow Girl caught her breath: the gesture felt like something a mother would do, though she no longer remembered for certain what that sensation might've been like.

The tension drained out of her body, and she felt the warmth beginning to creep back into her heart. It felt so kind that she once more thought she might start crying, though for the opposite reason this time.

"I'm a little slow," Arc Mage said. "Specifically, a little slow to regret thinking nothing of being slow."

"...Uh. So, so you..." Cow Girl groped for the words. "You're... the quest giver?"

"And a wizard and maybe a sage. It's hard to describe anyone in a single word."

"Uh-huh," Cow Girl said, not really understanding.

Not understanding at all, in fact—yet all the same, the meaning came through. So Cow Girl said "Uh-huh" again, and then, "Thank you."

"Thank me? After I hurt you so much? Even if it was accidental, though." Arc Mage gave Cow Girl a meaningful look and chuckled again. Even Cow Girl picked up on what she meant and went red up

to her ears. She realized now how embarrassing her behavior had been. She wished there was a hole she could crawl into.

"Come, come," Arc Mage said, unable to restrain another little burst of laughter. "I'll tell you a secret. Not to apologize, exactly. Just because. It's a special little something I just learned recently myself."

"...A secret..." Cow Girl blinked. "You mean magic?"

"All words are magic. Ready? He—"

He may seem dense and hard to talk to, but if you say something to him, he does listen.

A few minutes later, he came back, and Arc Mage left Cow Girl to go over to him. He nodded once to each of them, then said simply, "I'm off," and started walking.

Cow Girl saw them depart, then went over to the reception desk to finish the paperwork she'd forgotten about.

It must have been the heat of the summer morning.

All that Cow Girl remembered of her—of Arc Mage—was that one conversation.

Just that one simple memory.

OF HOW SHOWING OFF IS PART OF BEING AN ADVENTURER

"Okay, now." In the chatter-filled tavern, Spearman unrolled the quest paper he'd taken down. "This is our quest for today—make sense?"

"Let's, see…" The luscious beauty sitting across from him nodded wondrously. "It looks…rather…difficult, doesn't it?"

"Yeah, right?" Those breathy, halting words. Spearman nodded eagerly at her.

"A…warlock, I, see."

And so it was. Spearman sighed to himself. Any given spell caster was likely to be able to read and write, but…

Ugh. If she finds out I can't read, boy, will I look lame.

For the sake of his dignity, he had to hide the fact at any cost.

Naturally, even Spearman didn't want to just throw himself head-long into a random quest he'd found, with no idea what it entailed. Thus, he took his quest papers, not to the reception desk, but to the scribes, so they could read them to him.

This quest, allegedly, had to do with a warlock who had taken up residence in a cave near a village. He did bizarre experiments and cast hexes that caused the trees to rot and the animals to fall ill.

The quest had come from a village chieftain at the end of his rope, but Spearman was concerned. He didn't have a spell caster of his own, and that was dangerous.

Spearman was a warrior. He didn't know any magic. But he was all too aware of just how threatening a foe he faced.

Magic wasn't necessarily the only way to fight magic, but there was little substitute for knowledge and experience.

And he was in too deep now to turn back.

Most of today's quests were gone. Only a smattering of goblin-hunting ones were left. Spearman didn't want to be one of those buffoons who put a quest back on the board because he'd bitten off more than he could chew.

Come to think of it, I haven't seen that weirdo around today.

The adventurer in his grimy equipment would gladly have taken those goblin quests, Spearman suspected. He didn't have any idea what was so great about killing goblins, but that adventurer was set on his course of action.

"You're so strong, there's someone who would like to party up with you…"

The receptionist girl looked like an angel. No, a goddess! He had thought so ever since he first laid eyes on her. He couldn't be wrong.

He felt like things weren't bad between them. Even better, really: he thought they were quite good. He let the feeling carry him. He was on top of the world.

The one the receptionist had introduced him to had been the witch, the woman in front of him now. They'd worked together on more than one occasion before. She was beautiful. Great rack. Excellent all around.

"What, do you want to do…?"

"Er, r-right. Well, you don't *have* to use magic to kill him just because he's got magic, right?" The smile on Spearman's face was something of a bluff—*Fake it till you make it!* he thought. "Stab a guy with a spear and down he goes."

"Heh, heh…"

Witch gave a meaningful laugh at this. A sweet aroma seemed to accompany every breath she let out, perhaps the product of the tobacco she was always smoking. Spearman had no idea what it was, but he was just as glad she did it. Women like that were always more fun to talk to.

"Anyway, just leave it to me. We can work together, just like the time we stopped that Rock Eater, right?"

"I suppose, so…" She agreed with a slow, elegant nod.

And more importantly, we've worked together enough that I have a sense of who she is.

He wasn't so pathetic that he had to know every detail about a woman's background before he could talk to her. But after several adventures together, working as a team, they'd begun to trade jokes—it would be fair to call them friends.

Feeling as nervous as if he were going into battle right now, Spearman picked up his lemon water to calm his nerves.

"Say."

"Hrm?"

Witch's sudden interjection caught him completely off guard. He looked at her over the rim of his glass, but her expression was hidden beneath the brim of her hat.

"…Why…do you, always…talk, to…me?"

"No reason not to, right?" he answered immediately. He didn't hesitate at all. He hoped it communicated how silly he thought the question was.

"Is, that"—Witch blinked her long eyelashes—"because of, the way…I look…?"

"Doesn't hurt." Spearman nodded seriously. There wasn't a man in heaven or on earth who wouldn't praise the appearance of a beautiful woman. If he had been confronted with a mermaid, Spearman would have complimented her on the way her scales shimmered.

In fact, he found it the more attractive when a woman was aware of her own beauty.

"…" His answer must have surprised Witch, because her eyes opened wide.

I think she might be younger than I'd realized.

"…Hey, I can pretend not to notice if you want." Spearman suddenly felt embarrassed for some reason and tried to cover for himself.

"Then…" Witch swallowed, causing a gentle motion in her slim, pale throat. "My abilities, with magic?"

"Definitely part of it." Another serious nod.

How much of a coward did a man have to be to not acknowledge when a woman possessed a finely honed skill? Didn't matter if it was her beauty, her hair, or her clothes—or her swordsmanship, her learning, her faith, or even her magic.

"Gosh…" Witch pulled down her hat and slumped into her chair. "…Is there, anything else?"

Spearman grunted, then muttered, "Hold on," and looked at the ceiling.

The answer couldn't be no. It was just hard to put into words.

"…You remember we took the quest for that farm girl a while back?"

"Yes."

A nice, easy job, like going for a stroll. See one girl to a field somewhere, then get her home again.

Sure, it would have been dangerous for someone with no combat ability. That's why there'd been a quest, and why a couple of adventurers had taken it. But…

"It was boring, the reward sucked, but you went along with me without so much as pulling a face." Spearman spoke even as he organized his thoughts, finally concluding with, "Yeah, that's it… I thought you were good people."

"…I see."

Just that soft whisper, and then she took out her pipe slowly. She packed it with tobacco, struck a flint to it, took a puff.

"…I, don't view…myself as such…an easy woman…you understand?"

"But knowing someone appreciates your looks, your skills, and your heart—that's got to make you happy, right?"

Spearman grinned, showing his white teeth, a heartfelt smile.

Witch didn't say anything. She just shook her head, seemingly speechless.

©Shingo Adachi

CHAPTER 5

HER SCENARIO, HIS SCENARIO

"I'm curious—what was it you were talking about with that girl?"

A hawk screeched and circled overhead. Arc Mage, leading the way across the pathless field, glanced back.

Goblin Slayer, laden with cargo so heavy it forced his shoulders down, grunted under his helmet. "Nothing special," he said. Then he added, "I simply helped her with work."

Arc Mage smirked, took a dainty sip of the cider, and swallowed noisily. Her eyes were tender as she said, "That's not what I meant. I meant that witch."

"I requested her to do some work for me."

"Ah, that makes it all clear. And when you've got a perfectly good magical worker right here in front of you. Though I guess I am your quest giver."

Most lamentably, that leaves me unable to take on your requests.

Arc Mage giggled (was something funny?) and kept walking at a lively pace. Goblin Slayer, carrying the baggage, trod through the brush behind her.

Arc Mage didn't tell him where they were going. And Goblin Slayer didn't ask. There were goblins at her destination, and his job was to get rid of them. It didn't matter where they were headed. He didn't need to know anything except exactly what was required to do battle.

"Tell me, don't you ever get hot in that costume?" Arc Mage loosened the collar of her own shirt—deliberately, it seemed—and fanned at her cleavage. Of course, as far as Goblin Slayer could see, there wasn't a drop of sweat on her. The slight flush in her cheeks must have been from the alcohol. And even that was normal for her.

"No," Goblin Slayer responded briefly, then looked up at the sky.

The sunlight was strong, so bright it threatened to blind him. Summer must be nearly here. It would only get hotter.

"I think it's about time we found a place to camp for the night," Goblin Slayer said. Arc Mage nodded.

"Can't count on the wind in summer, can you?"

It was nearly the end of the second day since they'd left town.

§

"In the end, my quest for you is goblin slaying," Arc Mage said with a smile. It was night, and she was sitting by the bonfire Goblin Slayer had made. To avoid any risk of starting a wildfire, he had cut down nearby grass, then gathered up dry branches and grass and used them for fuel.

"Is that so?" Goblin Slayer replied as he put a skewer of cheese-covered sausage on the fire.

When the cheese had started to melt, Arc Mage pulled it back off, muttering "hot, hot, hot!" as she bit into it. "Mmmm…!" By the way the edges of her mouth turned up in pleasure, she seemed to like it.

Goblin Slayer, who had purchased the food almost at random, let out a small breath of relief.

"This comes from that farm, doesn't it? Did you do that on purpose?"

"The farm." Goblin Slayer looked down once more at the skewer in his hand. It was well cooked now—did they make this sort of thing on the farm? He bit into it, and the cheese was sweet, the sausage salted just right. One bite, then two, disappeared into his steel helmet. "I hadn't noticed."

"…Are you *that* type? The type that just wants to fill their stomachs and get some nutrition and doesn't care about anything else?"

Arc Mage made a face that said, *I can't believe it*, but he shook his head slowly from side to side.

"I am not picky, but my master taught me that if you want to stay alive, eat things that are warm and fatty."

"Ho," Arc Mage said, sounding impressed this time. "A personage of wide experience, it seems. Yes, I agree. If you have warm, fatty things, you can live."

"He was a rhea."

"Makes sense." Arc Mage nodded and put her lips to the opening of the bottle of cider as if it were the mouth of a lover. Then she licked up the droplets and gestured at him with the hand holding the bottle. "That's where we *get* the will to live. You eat what you want to eat."

"...What I want to eat?"

"Damn straight. No need to deny yourself." Arc Mage took a swallow of alcohol and a big bite of sausage as if to illustrate her point. "In that sense, I do wonder about the goblins."

"..."

Goblin Slayer didn't say anything, but picked up a good-sized stick and stirred the fire. When he looked closer, he saw that the stick was forked at the end. If one were to tie a rock there with some rope, it could be an excellent club.

"Are goblins happy, unhappy—? It must be easy, being completely ignorant, never thinking about anything."

"..."

"But then again, look how thin they are, how wasted with hunger. Their appetites are never satisfied. They're never full."

"I don't care," Goblin Slayer said. He almost spat the words. "The issue is what decisions they will make, how they will act. Not how they think about what's around them."

"Yes, indeed. You're absolutely right." Arc Mage tilted the bottle of alcohol toward her, loath to waste a single drop.

The fire crackled. Goblin Slayer stirred it again.

"That's why— Well, that's why I don't think it's wrong of you to decide not to write a book about goblins."

That was likely the reason he managed not to miss the last of her whispers. And it was probably to blame for why he couldn't see her expression, either.

"The pursuit of knowledge isn't a happy one. It takes such effort. First to obtain it, and then to live with it.

"And most people don't even want it in the first place," she added.

"People don't want dry histories of heroes—they want romantic ballads."

Goblin Slayer nodded. He had a sense of what she meant. He remembered, back in his own village, hearing a number of stories of heroes. Each had probably been mangled by the bard who sang it. But he had believed them and dreamed he would become an adventurer—or at least, that he wanted to be.

But he never could be. It simply wasn't possible.

"Even the Monster Manual is like that. Look how hard we're working, eh? And we're hardly the only ones."

Learning, researching, writing, editing. Arc Mage's words seemed to dance through the night air.

Collating, binding, transport, delivery, reception, and storage…

The knowledge of how to do all those things was itself the great precondition to the production of the book.

"And that knowledge"—Arc Mage spoke with the mercilessness of someone cutting open the belly of a living thing out of absolute necessity—"we have no obligation to share for free with some kid who runs away from his village, can't even read, and gets himself killed hunting goblins."

Even if they were told, they wouldn't have either the inclination or the capacity to understand what they were hearing.

That's learning for you.

"So you won't write a goblin book? Purely from the perspective of cost versus benefit, you're absolutely right."

Goblin Slayer thought for a moment. There had been a temple of the God of Knowledge in his village. A small one, but still… Looking back now, he wished he had gone to it more often. As it stood, he had no education other than the basic letters his sister had taught him.

"…I thought adherents of the God of Knowledge were passionate about spreading learning and study."

"Yes, about gaining and sharing it. Their ideal world would be bounteous and kind and peaceful and sounds wonderful."

Goblin Slayer thought again. A world where anyone and everyone had access to knowledge. He couldn't imagine it. Reading and writing were one thing, but knowledge wasn't something one was simply given.

Neither simply given, nor simply gained, he thought.

"But our world isn't ideal, not by a long shot. It's the gods' tabletop, overflowing with fate and chance."

I've got no sympathy for people who go ignorantly to their deaths. Not when I don't even know their faces.

Thus, Arc Mage murmured—maybe she didn't even especially intend for him to hear—and then once again put her lips lovingly to her cider bottle.

"The light of knowledge is thin, and the darkness of ignorance still o'erweening."

"..."

"Your own knowledge might be one spark against that darkness."

The words caused Goblin Slayer to move his helmet slightly, to look in her direction. In between the darkness of the night and the glow of the fire, he thought he could just see her eyes brimming.

Maybe it was an illusion. "Then," he asked, "what about yours?"

She didn't answer...except for the hint of an ambiguous smile that he caught just beyond the flames.

§

"And so we've come to a corner," she said as they reached the edge of the field. The brush thinned out beneath their feet, bare earth becoming visible.

There was a wilderness ahead. A wasteland. The earth here was a dirty red color, as if seared by a flame; some said it was the aftermath of a great battle from the Age of the Gods.

That didn't interest Goblin Slayer. He said only, "I see."

"About one out of every four directions will yield one, in broad terms. Of course, it doesn't have to be four."

And once again, he repeated, "I see." He did, however, add, "Is that our destination?"

"In a manner of speaking, yes.

"*For example,*" she said, giving a shake of her hand. She produced a die, the flourish unnatural, as if she were doing magic.

The die sparkled like the fang of a beast, or like a treasure. It caught the red light of the sun and scattered it everywhere.

"How many corners does this die have?"

"Eight."

"Excellent. And faces?"

"Six."

"Another superb answer."

Now... Arc Mage gave an alluring smile, as if to an especially talented student. "If you come to one of those corners, what do you see?"

"..." Goblin Slayer thought for a second. Then he stated a simple fact. "Three faces, I suppose."

"Indubitably!" Arc Mage smiled as if he had guessed exactly what she was thinking.

She didn't appear to be aware of any danger, even though she was walking backward. Goblin Slayer adjusted the load on his shoulders and walked behind her, which was to say, in front of her.

"When you aspire to reach the top of a mountain, is the summit your true destination? Or the view? Or what's beyond? That's the question."

"I see," Goblin Slayer said for the third time. "So there are goblins there."

"We finally found it, and look. It's enough to make a girl's heart break."

Have a look.

Arc Mage spoke almost as if she could see behind herself, then turned around with a smile.

Goblin Slayer hadn't noticed until she called his attention to it.

A dark tower. A great, looming shadow in the gloom.

It stood tall over the wasteland, reaching up to the sky.

He blinked behind his visor. Then he grunted. "...I missed it."

"Not surprising. Only people who know about it can see it."

Goblin Slayer nodded disinterestedly, then crouched down and looked closely at the tower's entrance.

Yes, there they are.

Goblins moved like stains of ink against the shadows. Guards, most likely. They carried short spears and stood vacantly at their posts, looking tired.

"Thinking alone won't tell us what in the world they're doing here," a voice whispered in his ear. He caught the faint whiff of cider and medicine.

Behind his visor, Goblin Slayer dropped his eyes, taking in Arc Mage where she leaned on his shoulder.

"I wonder if there was some kind of battle to the east. To bring the shades of the goblins' deaths all the way out here."

"Shades...?" He didn't know this word very well.

Noticing his uncertainty, Arc Mage simply said, "I'll explain later," and laughed. "The easy way would be to climb the outer walls or fly through the air to make for the top, but I guess we can't do that."

"Climb the outer walls," he echoed softly.

I see. That's one possibility.

"...So we will go through the inside?"

"Yep. C'mon."

Arc Mage twisted as if pulling out of a man's grasp, coming off his shoulder. She still had the same pregnant grin on her face as always. She asked him, "What will you do?"

He answered. There was only one answer. No need to hesitate.

"I will kill all the goblins."

It was clear what had to be done.

And where.

The only question…was *how*.

§

With the tower looming before them, the adventurer and his quest giver watched and waited for their chance.

Goblins grunted and growled at the entrance. There were no trees around the tower; the guards would be able to see for quite a distance.

There was just a single rosebush, large enough for two people to conceal themselves. Once they got past it, the goblins were sure to notice them.

"…There's no shadow," Goblin Slayer said softly. The sinking sun was falling behind the tower, wreathing it in darkness, but the tower itself cast no shadow. It should have been impossible unless the sun were at its zenith—no, even then.

"So it will be difficult for us to hide as we approach."

Naturally, Goblin Slayer wasn't concerned with such trivial details for their own sake. Then too, since goblins could see in the dark, he didn't know whether hiding in the shadows really helped. Regardless, a full frontal assault without so much as an attempt at something better bothered him.

"Look close. The goblins don't cast shadows either, right?" Arc Mage's voice was fast and high-pitched; she made no effort to hide her excitement. "That's because it's *all* shadows. Shades can't cast shadows. It only makes sense. See what I'm saying?"

"No," he said bluntly. It came out as a soft grunt. "I don't understand what these shades are that you keep talking about."

"They're what spell casters chase." Arc Mage grinned, although Goblin Slayer saw nothing funny and remained silent. "I told you. Thinking about it won't get you anywhere. They've respawned from some battle somewhere."

"…"

"Meaning, just like the tower, the shades of those goblins are being cast from somewhere. For example…" She gave Goblin Slayer a pointed glance. "That green moon you talked about, say."

"…So can we kill them?"

©Shingo Adachi

Arc Mage gave him an amorous wink. Then she chuckled, like when a child manages to correctly guess the answer; she sounded quite amused. "Things with no shadows lack something in life force. They're flat, front and back the same. I won't say there's no way you can kill a shadow."

"So we can kill them." Goblin Slayer focused on the only part of that speech he understood, and this was the conclusion he drew from it. Otherwise, there would have been no point in his quest giver dragging him all this way out here.

Yes. Arc Mage nodded. "You know how we say 'to shadow'? To imitate? It cuts both ways. What we do to the shade affects the thing that casts it. We can take advantage of the identification with the true tower..."

Then Arc Mage murmured, *"I guess there's no real point in discussing this,"* and smiled.

"Well, think of it like a hex. Step on a goblin's shadow, and he'll die. It's the same logic."

"I understand," Goblin Slayer said. He didn't know anything about hexes. "That will do, then."

There was only one thing that mattered.

He couldn't understand this tower that had appeared out of nowhere, nor the goblins Arc Mage called shades.

"What you are saying is, those goblins can be killed."

His next actions were swift as the wind. Once he knew what to do, there was no reason to hesitate.

Goblin Slayer picked up some small stones lying in the wasteland, choosing the most well formed of them.

"Here I go."

Even as he spoke, he was flinging the stone, then drawing his sword and rushing in.

The goblin guard spotted him kicking his way out of the rosebush and opened his mouth.

The stone flew toward him as if it had been waiting for this moment, smacking him in the brain stem and throwing him backward before he could shout.

"GOROBBG?!"

"One...!"

The other guard tried to raise his spear, but Goblin Slayer slammed full into him.

"GBB! GROBG!!"

He deflected the crude spear tip with his shield, then slashed across the throat with his sword.

"GRBBO?!"

A dim geyser of blood arced through the twilight, staining the steel helmet.

"That's two."

He pulled out his sword and shook off the blood, drove it into the throat of the other, still-twitching, goblin, and said, "…If they bleed, then I agree. We can kill them."

Everything about them, right up to the way they felt under his blade, was like real goblins. And the corpses didn't vanish, either. Being shades or shadows or whatever else seemed to make scant difference, and that was just as well. A goblin was a goblin.

He wiped the blood and fat on one of the monsters' loincloths, then picked up a short spear. Again, be it a shadow or whatever, as long as this weapon was real enough, it was no inconvenience to him.

"We'll go inside before we're noticed. Come on."

"Sheesh, always in a hurry, you are… Ooh, wait just a second."

At his summons, Arc Mage tried to stand up from her place among the roses, making the bush rustle. Jogging carefully so as not to tread on the flowers, she came over and reached out to one of the goblin corpses.

He thought she was about to pull out that curved knife, but he was wrong.

"No time here. This will have to do for a disguise." She chuckled and doused her fingers in the blood, smearing it onto her face in complicated patterns that looked like letters. When Goblin Slayer caught a whiff, it smelled to him like fresh ink.

"Is that some kind of spell?"

"Call it Flavor Text. Come on, let's go!"

Goblin Slayer nodded, and they passed through the entrance to the dark tower.

§

I've never seen anything like it, but it just seems to repeat itself, Goblin Slayer thought as they worked their way through the tessellated tunnel with an item whose purpose he didn't understand.

Inside, the tower was like an especially convoluted maze. Was it made of metal? The passages went on and on seamlessly, no windows, barely large enough for the two of them to walk abreast.

Before they had entered, he had thought they might need a torch, but although there was no visible source of light, it was surprisingly easy to see inside. For some reason, though, everything always faded into darkness at a set distance ahead of them. He had tried lobbing a lit torch into the gloom, but nothing changed, so he simply accepted that this was the way things worked here.

"Your ability to take things for what they are is one of your virtues." Arc Mage laughed, but...

The most important thing was that they hadn't yet run into a large crowd of goblins, but he didn't like wasting time in transit.

"Six...!"

"GBBOR?!"

Goblin Slayer smashed the edge of his shield into the nose of a goblin who was coming around the corner. It shattered the nose, stabbed into the brain, and the goblin fell back and expired, a bloody mess.

The brain is a vital point, even for a goblin. Such was the conclusion he had come to after a great deal of fighting, reflection, investigation, and analysis.

There was something to gain from each goblin he slaughtered, whether it was theoretical knowledge or practical skill. All was reference, all was practice, and all was experience.

"Seven!"

This, for example.

Goblin Slayer hefted the spear in his hand and flung it as hard as he could down the passageway. It stabbed through the air, then through the chest of a goblin, delivering another fatal wound.

He jumped on the gasping, blood-vomiting creature, breaking its neck.

"Your throws are getting better and better." *Hee-hee.* From a step or two behind him, Arc Mage restrained her laughter as she spoke.

"Being able to take the initiative and attack anywhere, in a room or a hallway or wherever else—that makes you strong."

And unlike a bow and arrow, he didn't need two hands to do it.

Goblin Slayer nodded at this, then picked up a club from one of the goblins. "Do you know where we are going? If we get lost, we'll be in trouble."

"No worries on that score," Arc Mage said, making a broad and elegant gesture with her left hand. On it was the crackling glimmer of Spark.

"This will be our guide—or maybe I should say, wherever I go, that's where we want to be."

"I don't understand."

"The destination isn't chosen by the spark but by its master."

Just keep going. Goblin Slayer heeded Arc Mage's words.

Despite several forks and a few chambers, the scenery never changed. The room they finally arrived at looked just like all the others, the only difference being a thick door amid all that empty space.

No, there was another difference as well…

"What is this?"

Something like mist floated in front of the door, which appeared as if made of ebony and had no keyhole.

Goblin Slayer ignored it at first, inspecting the door. It was good that it didn't have a keyhole. But although it seemed like two doors that would open in the middle, there was no seam at the center.

"Hmm… That would appear to make this the center of it all," Arc Mage said, sounding at once amused and concerned as she started prodding at the mist. Each time she did so, the black haze would shift in its shape, jumping and popping like a bubble. "The true body that's lost its form by casting this shadow… In other words, I think this is the key."

"Can you do anything about it?"

"We just need to get this thing back into its proper form… I think?"

"I don't know," Goblin Slayer replied, looking back the way they had come.

He heard the gibbering voices of goblins. Maybe they had finally noticed something was wrong.

Then there were stamping footsteps, and then more chattering. The sound of a medley of equipment smacking one against another.

Under his helmet, he let out a breath. This would be relatively easy. No enemies behind, just the one entrance ahead. Much simpler than defending a village. This was a fight he couldn't afford to lose—but that was as it always was. Nor was there any change in what he had to do.

"I'll leave that to you."

"Yes, well, I'll give it the old college try," she said bravely from behind him, and meanwhile, he met the first goblin to jump through the entrance with his club.

"GOBORO?!"

"Hmph."

The monster's skull shattered, spraying bone and blood and brains everywhere.

Goblin Slayer slammed the club into two or three more before he tossed it away and dropped into a deep stance.

The grimy leather armor, the cheap-looking steel helmet. On his left arm was tied a small round shield, while in his right hand was a sword of a strange length.

"GOB! GOOBBG!!"

"This makes ten!"

As the goblin shouted and flew at him, he swept his blade upward to catch him under the chin.

"GOBOGO?!"

The monster's twitching corpse smacked into its neighbor as it landed.

Without missing a beat, Goblin Slayer used his shield to catch the club swung by a goblin on the left, then swept, ignoring the numbness in his arm.

"Eleven…!" When the monster stumbled, he jammed his sword into its throat. Blood came gushing out, polluting the hilt and his hand. Goblin Slayer immediately let go of the sword, taking an ax from the now-dead goblin as he kicked the corpse away.

The goblins had shoved aside the body of the first monster he had killed and were closing in from the front.

"Hrm…!"

He deflected a spear with his shield, dealt out a blow with his ax. He gave no thought to restraint. The slaughter of them all was his only goal.

"The enemy wants you dead! You think you can win when you don't care if you hit them or not?"

Thus said his master, while raining down a flurry of blows upon him.

Draw your sword with the intent to kill, and think of restraint only after.

Goblin Slayer took a deep breath, steadying his breathing; he pulled out the ax he had buried in a goblin's head.

"Ten, and two."

"GOROBG..."

"GBBB...!"

The goblins, unsure how to press the attack, growled hatefully at him.

At this distance, smell could no longer cover for anything.

A woman. There's a woman there. A young woman. And it's just the two of them. Take. Steal.

The goblins made hideous faces, full of lust and hatred. Shades they may have been, but they were still goblins. Perhaps that made them worse.

They had found a woman at last, and they were frustrated to discover their way blocked. Yes, they were the ones trying to attack her, but that didn't give this adventurer the right to stop them.

If only *he* weren't there. This was *his* fault.

"GRRGB! GBGOROGOB!"

"GOROGG!"

Goblin Slayer didn't understand the goblin language. But somehow, he seemed to understand what the band of goblins was thinking all too easily.

Now, how to kill them?

His hand went to his ax as he thought, *Let them come.* The narrow entryway would keep them from ambushing him and hamper the effect of their numbers, and in a one-on-one fight with a goblin, he couldn't lose.

At least, not so long as his strength held out...

"...What in the world?"

This confidence kept him from feeling much concern even when he heard Arc Mage mutter in surprise behind him.

"This is wrong, this isn't right...!"

"What is it?"

"This sort of corporeal body isn't supposed to exist! It's not structurally possible!"

"I see."

He'd never heard her sound so perplexed, or so worried, before.

But why should he think that he could understand anything, let alone everything, about another person?

"I can still hold them off," he said. "For a while."

"Yeah, I know… Believe me, I know…!"

He could hear her biting her thumbnail. But he was more interested in the actions of the goblins, who had begun to smile viciously when they heard the woman's voice.

"GGOBOGOBG!!"

A leap.

Perhaps the monster was trying to jump over not just the corpse of his companion, but even Goblin Slayer's head.

Goblin Slayer gave a deep sigh. He had plenty of strength left.

"GOROR?!"

"Thirteen."

He knew one goblin weak point: right between the legs.

He delivered a merciless ax blow to that point.

"GOBOGOBOGOOBO?!?!"

The goblin gave an earsplitting howl, his eyes rolling back in his head as he twitched and thrashed.

"GOROB?!"

"Fourteen… Hrm."

The goblin screamed and fell backward, trying to extract the dagger from his eye, and there expired.

Goblin Slayer nodded. So the eyes were soft.

"That makes them vulnerable."

Sometime, he would have to come up with a way of blinding them. That was, if there was a sometime.

He kicked a weapon from the goblin writhing at his feet into his hand.

"GOROG! GGBOROGO!"

"GOOROGBG!!"

The din of battle continued. Arc Mage, meanwhile, frowned her handsome features, sweat and tears running down her face as she worked at the mist.

It was indeed just like fog: try to catch hold of it, and you found yourself grasping empty air.

But so what?

That was no different from everything else.

No different from everything she had achieved until now, everything she had obtained.

She crouched on the floor, pulling a blackboard and chalk out of her bag. She began writing numbers furiously.

All was numbers. Data was made of numbers.

If the gods themselves were data, then even they could be understood, figured out. It had to be possible.

One, two. Goblin Slayer continued to produce his pile of goblin corpses. In time with him, her brilliant brain began tying ambiguous things together, one, two.

"...I see, I get it! I understand! It all...makes...sense!!"

The cheer of triumph came when there were perhaps another ten dead goblins on the ground. Arc Mage threw aside the chalkboard, taking up the deck of cards she'd assembled into a spell book.

"A projection of a higher dimension! It's like drawing on paper—in other words, *this* is the shadow!"

She gave a powerful tap to the floor of the dark tower as she stood. Then she turned over the cards in her hand, and with the whirlwind of magical powers that came welling up, she set upon the mist.

"Three vertices, three lines. Four vertices, four faces. And if so, then one dimension higher, the smallest figure!"

The words, like a spell, came fluently, slamming into the black fog one after another, turning them back from nothingness, changing them like a blooming flower.

"...Meaning five vertices, five cells!"

Clack. There was a sound as of something activating.

Immediately, a single line appeared down the ebony door, a line of light that ran as if carved with a sword.

Here openeth the dark tower!

"YYYEEESSS!!" Arc Mage exclaimed in a voice that could have passed for a hunting horn. "Once you understand it, it's nothing! Child's play! Goblin Slayer!!"

"...Yes."

He was in the middle of attacking his twenty-sixth goblin, jamming the broken tip of a short spear into the monster's eye. When he pulled the spear back out, the eyeball came with it, ocular nerve and all. Goblin Slayer threw the whole thing away, spun on his heel, and started running.

"GORO! GGBGOGOB!!"

"GOROGB!!"

With the impediment suddenly removed, the goblins rushed into the room like a dark flood.

"Can you close the door, too?!" Goblin Slayer demanded.

"Of course I can! Who do you think I—?"

"Then do it...!"

Goblin Slayer grabbed Arc Mage up in his arms, ignoring her little yelp.

"Gah! You know, I think your treatment of women could use some refinement, you—!"

"Just do it now!"

Ignoring every objection and complaint, Goblin Slayer jumped directly through the door. Behind him, he could hear the gibbering, slavering goblins closing in.

"I know, I know, you don't have to shout," Arc Mage groused from his shoulder. She made a motion with her fingers. In response, the black mist roiled and changed shape.

"GOROOGGB!!"

One goblin reached out, trying to force his way through the door—but it was too late.

"You lot...are *not* invited."

The ebony portal closed without a sound, locking.

The only thing left was a lone goblin arm, lying on the ground like a chopped nut.

§

"…So what, exactly, was that?" Goblin Slayer asked as they climbed a seemingly endless spiral staircase.

On the other side of the door was a set of stairs that corkscrewed around and around, so far it seemed like it might go on forever. Judging by the height of the tower, though, that was only natural, and neither the adventurer nor the quest giver complained.

Goblin Slayer, though, certainly didn't voice the question from an inability to stand the silence.

"Mm, well," Arc Mage said, puffing out her chest like a proud child. "It was a shade. Those who live in a world of lines and faces can't comprehend height. We're not so different, ourselves…"

We know length, width, and height, but add another axis that springs from an additional dimension…

Still, there was a knowing grin on her face. "…But we can see the shadow the thing casts and tease it out. If we know how, that is."

"So that was that strange object."

"You got it."

"Can the goblins break through it?"

Hmm. She stopped, leaning against the wall for support. Goblin Slayer stopped as well, looking back at her.

"Well," she said, nodding, "I understand what you're asking, but strictly speaking, the answer is no."

"It's impossible for them?"

"Not impossible. But it's possible in the same way it would be possible for a monkey to write a novel by scrawling random letters."

Or like a random encounter with a dragon. Goblin Slayer grunted softly.

The chance was greater than zero. That fact could inspire courage, or concern. By chance or by fate, what would happen would happen. To hell with the rest.

"Then answer what I was actually asking."

"If you meant are there goblins up ahead, the answer is certainly." Arc Mage gave a wave of her hand as if she were tossing a ball. "Those are shades, remember. You glance up, and poof, there they are. You can't fathom where they come from."

"Is that so?"

"Even I was surprised."

She gave her cider bottle a loving pat, then one of those kisses, drinking noisily from it. *Phew!* She let out a warm breath then wiped her mouth with the back of her hand.

"I finally get a fix on my destination, and it turns out to be a goblin nest."

"That happens often." Then Goblin Slayer elaborated quietly: "Very often."

"I wonder if we should chalk that up to fate, or to chance. It's a puzzle."

"I don't care."

"You're no fun." Arc Mage laughed aloud. Goblin Slayer ignored her, taking the next step, then the next.

If there were goblins here, then he had to focus on being ready for them. Everything else was trivial.

He pulled a stamina potion out of his bag, drinking it down in a single gulp the way Arc Mage drank her cider. There was no telling how high this tower was, how long the fight with the goblins would continue—so perhaps he should have nursed it a bit at a time.

"Well, you don't need to worry about anything other than goblins," Arc Mage said, jogging up behind him, and she sounded very confident. "If this tower is for us, then that amorphous thing is my obstacle… In a word, the shade of a god."

"A god."

"What you might call an avatar or a spirit. It's not easy to grasp the form of a deity. My mathematical formulas might even count as divine, you see?"

A god.

Goblin Slayer didn't look back. The word felt so far from him.

It wasn't a goblin, and that meant it was of no interest.

§

Arc Mage, indeed, was as good as her word.

"Yes… Yes, yes!" She challenged the gods' froth on the next level as well and achieved a brilliant victory. "When you know the rules and the formulae, the rest is calculation! Try that on for size! …Yes, I'm sure about this!"

The blackboard and chalk had been summarily abandoned back on the second level. Now Arc Mage simply put a finger to her chin, muttered to herself for a moment, and then exclaimed, "It's eight!"

The amorphous foam reversed, shining like stars as it formed into a key that then opened the door forward. Goblin Slayer, who had been defending them against the encroaching goblins, immediately hefted Arc Mage up and ran through.

"I thought I told you to learn some manners!"

"Not interested."

All was repetition. On the third level, and the fourth, she didn't even bother pretending to calculate. She would simply give the floor a hard tap with her foot then use the magic that swelled up to control her cards, opening the door on the spot.

"Sixteen—," it was, and then, "—Twenty-four!"

And even so, it was like magic.

Thankfully, it allowed Goblin Slayer to conserve a considerable amount of his strength. The goblins' aggression didn't seem to wane for having to climb the stairs. And if he couldn't wipe them out all at once, then he would just have to keep up the work individually.

He changed tactics, changed equipment, changed weapons, used every bit of his knowledge, relied on practiced movements, then switched to something different. He slashed throats, gouged eyeballs, split skulls, spilled viscera, smashed faces. The less work it took, the better.

From that perspective, the fifth floor could be called just a bit of trouble.

"Hrm, hrm, hrm… Well now, this sure is something else."

"Is it difficult?" Goblin Slayer asked, stepping on the neck of his hundred and second—or was that hundred and third?—goblin.

"GOROOG! GBBGR!"

"GRB!"

His shoulders heaved with his breath. He fought to get his breathing under control then smashed another goblin with his shield. Despite a brief rest and some potions, the fatigue was undeniably building. The delving of massive, complex labyrinths was the work of powerful, Gold- or Platinum-ranked adventurers. Goblin Slayer, still among the lower ranks, had never imagined himself in such a world.

But it is still better than the fight in the village, he concluded, thinking back to a defensive battle he had once fought, single-handedly covering an entire settlement.

This was nothing. Compared to that fight, here he had only to worry about what was in front of him. And it wasn't raining.

Just one person to protect. Fresh weapons being brought to him by his own enemies. The only issues were strength and focus.

"Difficult! Now, there's a word!" Arc Mage let up a howl of her own.

Difficult? Difficult, you say? Do you know who you're talking to? She glared at the shade of the higher dimension with the look of a general surveying a battlefield then put her cards to work.

"Just you look at this! A hundred and twenty? I could bring that together with one hand tied behind my back!"

The thin air bubbled up, blossomed, and flowered into a key. The key turned in the lock. The door split silently in two. Arc Mage gave a triumphant chuckle. "The way has been opened! Let's go—we've no time to dally with goblins!"

Goblin Slayer didn't answer but only said, "One hundred and five," as he stabbed a goblin in the neck.

"GOOBGGRGRG?!"

The monster screamed and fell back; Goblin Slayer let the sword go, picking up a club at his feet.

"It is not easy to annihilate them all."

"I told you, they'll keep on spawning forever! But we have limited resources!"

Goblin Slayer gave a click of his tongue and turned quickly. Arc Mage appeared to have learned from experience; she was already heading through the door.

"I don't ever want you lugging me around again!" she exclaimed as Goblin Slayer followed after her.

"GOOBGRG!"

"GB! GBOOR!"

The goblins jabbered behind them, but then the door shut tight, locking them out.

They were once again at the bottom of a massive spiral staircase. Goblin Slayer let out a deep breath.

"I don't like it."

"What don't you like?" Arc Mage asked, looking puzzled as she made to start climbing the stairs. She took a small, reluctant sip of her remaining cider, the bottle now mostly empty.

"The thought of what would happen if these goblins got out of this tower."

"Ha-ha-ha-ha-ha. And here I thought you were worrying about how to get home."

Goblin Slayer shook his head. The only directions to go were up and down; the job at hand would not change.

"Well, don't sweat it. They only exist inside the shade of the tower."

"So they can't leave it?"

"And when the sun goes down, shadows disappear. They're only here when the tower is. Most likely…" She looked up the stairs with a dreamy expression. "…when I arrive, that'll be the end of it."

"I see," he said curtly.

Arc Mage looked at him in exasperation then laughed aloud. She put her hands on her stomach, almost rolling around, reminding him of the first time they'd met.

"You really are a special one! Aren't you curious at all about what's in here or what I'm trying to do?"

"That doesn't interest me," he said, shaking his head. "Or…"

Arc Mage had settled herself on the stairs and rested her chin in her hands, eagerly awaiting what he would say next.

Goblin Slayer gave one of those quiet grunts of his then went on softly, "…My teacher told me that all things come down to *do* or *do not*."

"A rhea teacher," Arc Mage said, squinting. "He didn't say *success or failure*?"

"Success and failure both come about because of doing. If you do not, they never occur."

This was the first time he had said this to anybody. He didn't understand why he had chosen to say it now.

I believe it, he whispered. *I didn't do it. Didn't attempt it. That's why.*

"I don't question what other people decide to do."

"As long as it doesn't get in the way of killing goblins, you mean?"

"That's right."

Arc Mage nodded. She looked genuinely, profoundly happy. "Now I know getting you for my quests was the right choice, Goblin Slayer."

"Is that so?"

"Heh!" She gave a nasal chuckle then got lightly to her feet. "All right, let's go! Your quest giver's destination is just up ahead, dear adventurer!"

Do you really know that? To Goblin Slayer's inquiry, Arc Mage replied that of course she did.

"Four, six, eight, twelve, twenty. These five are the basis for the shapes of things as we know them."

They climbed the stairs, going into a hallway out of which goblins poured. They silenced their footsteps, silenced their breathing, and, finally, silenced the goblins, proceeding ever deeper.

It was a different level, and the details varied subtly, but the layout was basically the same as all the others. They were obviously aiming for a chamber in the center of the tower, and quest giver and adventurer alike proceeded without hesitation.

In fact, so long as Spark shined on her finger, there would be no hesitation.

"So far, the shadows cast into this tower have been five, eight, sixteen, twenty-four, and one hundred and twenty."

"Five of them." Goblin Slayer brought his hand around at a goblin behind him, slashing the monster's throat. There was a whistling sound and a geyser of blood. He waited until the creature was dead then cast the corpse away.

"That's why I think we've hit the end here. I think five should work again."

"Is that so?"

"To be fair, we won't know for sure until we try…"

In any event, it was just as she said.

There was the ebony door in what was presumably the final room—and before it, again, a shadow. Arc Mage frowned. "I hate to admit it, but I've miscalculated," she said. "But anyway, the principle's the same. We'll manage."

"Is that so?" Goblin Slayer nodded. "Then I will keep doing my job."

"GOOBOGR! GOOROG!"

"GGOBOGOB!!"

Even the voices of the goblins coming up from behind were the same. Goblin Slayer forced his body, growing ever heavier, to move, taking up a position to defend the door. He produced another stamina potion from his bag. Not many left now. He gulped it down.

"GOROOGB!"

"…I've lost track of the numbers." He clicked his tongue and pitched the bottle away. It smashed open along with the skull of the goblin it hit, and the battle began. "That's one."

"Add one hundred five and twelve to that," Arc Mage said without turning around. Goblin Slayer *harrumph*ed softly.

"One hundred eighteen."

Then he swung the club in his hand, slamming it into the next goblin.

"GOOBOG?!"

"That's one hundred nineteen!"

§

Slice the goblins, stab them, hit them, strike them, fling things at them, and, finally, kill them.

"GGOBOGR?!"

"GOOGRB! GBOG!!"

In a word, Goblin Slayer went about producing a mountain of corpses.

No matter how many he murdered in that narrow entranceway, no matter how many bodies piled up, their aggression never waned. Was it because they were shades, or simply because they were goblins? The attackers merely used the corpses of their fellows as shields, flinging stones from behind them.

"………Hrm."

The rocks bounced off his shield and his helmet with a dull popping sound. His arm was numb. He had to fight to hold his head up. A hit to his shoulder had gone through the armor to his flesh, and now he was slower to move his shield.

"Ohh, ah!!"

"GOROOBG!!"

One goblin saw his chance and came rushing out from behind the barrier. Goblin Slayer tossed his sword, which had nearly slipped out of his hand, at the monster, keeping him at bay. He staggered backward with the sword lodged in his throat, coughing up blood until he tumbled to the ground.

Happily for Goblin Slayer, he had an armory's worth of weapons there at his feet. He kicked a club up into his hand, almost groaning as he tried to even out his breath. The goblins understood well how to use their numbers to their advantage; whether this was instinctive or deliberate, he didn't know. They would try to rush forward and take all the glory, or use their foolish compatriots as decoys.

It was not that the goblins didn't fear death. Each was simply, albeit baselessly, certain that he alone among the horde would not die.

As the onslaught continued, Goblin Slayer's strength began to ebb. The battle to get here had been nothing compared to the war he was waging now. It was his experience defending that village which allowed him to make the jump to this battle.

In that case, he'd had plenty of time to establish defenses. If only he could have built some kind of barricade right now.

I don't have enough hands.

They were only goblins. The weakest of all monsters. No matter how hard they fought, that fact remained.

But the sheer quantity of them could be enough to bring low a party of adventurers. Let alone a single adventurer all by himself.

Goblin Slayer had learned that lesson by now. Whether he would live to make use of it was another question.

"Damn… What the hell is wrong here?!"

The situation wasn't lost on Arc Mage. She was smart enough. She had to understand. And that only made her the more panicked. Sweat dripped down her brow.

Desperately wracking her brain to deal with her own foe, the shadow floating in the air, she was faced with one cruel fact.

"...It's going to take too much time!"

She knew.

She understood.

She knew what this meant—and she knew all too well.

"This goes beyond the hundred and twenty earlier. This... This is *six hundred*!"

A six-hundred polychoron—an entity that easily surpassed anything Arc Mage had imagined.

She could fathom it. She could imagine it.

And yet, even yet, how much time would it take to calculate it?

How much time had she spent getting here?

How much time offering her life to the game board, meeting her master, honing her knowledge, running this way and that—

"Still not enough time...?!"

Her vision blurred. She knew. It wasn't that she was bitter or sad. It was just the natural byproduct of heightened emotions, or so she kept telling herself. And thus, she didn't even give herself the time to wipe the tears from her eyes but continued her challenge to divine providence.

For the same reason, Goblin Slayer had to buy them every minute, every second he could.

"GOROBBG?!"

"Oh-hh—!!"

How many now? He had forgotten the number she'd told him earlier.

His breath came in ragged gasps. The oxygen wasn't reaching his brain.

Was it his master who had guffawed and informed him that his brain was only useful for making snot?

And no one ever died from a lack of snot...

"GBB! GOROBG!"

"...Feh!"

Something struck his foot. A goblin had crawled through the mountain of corpses and brought a dagger down on it.

Try as he might to count the number of kills, but in the midst of this battle, he could hardly make sure it actually tallied up with the number of corpses.

Of course, Goblin Slayer was ready for this; he made sure to protect his feet. The blade didn't touch his body.

He did, however, feel his footing grow unsteady: goblin blood. He shifted his hip to catch himself, and that was when the goblins pressed in.

"GOBB!"

"GROGGB! GROB!!"

"Ahh!!"

He gritted his teeth and rolled sideways, lashing out with his club. A couple of goblins he caught in the shin yelped and fell down. A third goblin went tumbling over them.

Goblin Slayer felt a shock of fear. He couldn't allow them past him. Must not let them get to her.

One goblin made a beeline for the defenseless woman behind the adventurer, probably making some hideous face. Goblin Slayer slapped the floor tiles, stretching himself out.

An impact at his back. Other goblins in the way. He ignored them.

Then he let go of his club and grabbed the goblin's foot with his right hand. He had hold of it. He pulled.

"Hrr—ahhh!"

"GBBBOR?!"

The shield in his left hand flashed up toward the back of the head. The edge of the shield split the head, and blood came gushing out.

He didn't have even a second to spare. The goblins were pressing in. A weapon. He needed a weapon...

"I've...got one...!"

He lifted up the still-twitching goblin corpse. Then, using it like a shield, he slammed it into the horde of enemies.

"GOOBOGR?!"

"GOOB?!"

Quantity would always have certain advantages, but so would quality.

The armor-clad adventurer added his own weight to that of the corpse as he shoved. He slammed into several goblins at once, pushing them back outside the chamber.

"Hrr, uh…!"

Goblin Slayer let out a great breath, noticing the fresh pool of blood forming beneath him. The dull ache in his back was not, it seemed, from a club or other blunt weapon. He reached around behind himself to find an ax had shattered his armor and wounded him in the back. Perfect. This was a weapon.

He pulled it out, ignoring the flow of blood. A stunning pain lanced through him, but he held his breath and bore it.

"How much…longer?" There was the slightest quaver in his voice as he asked the question.

"I don't… I don't know…!" The strangled response sounded to Goblin Slayer like the speaker might burst into tears at any moment. "I can solve it. I can tease it out. I *will*. But—but I just don't have enough…*time*!!"

Goblin Slayer took a breath in, let it out.

"You don't?"

"No…! Damn! To come this far, all for… Arrgh, damn it all…"

Arc Mage stopped talking for a moment. She took a few hesitant, shallow breaths, as if unsure whether to say anything further.

Then she spoke.

"This was supposed to be *my* scenario, *my* adventure. I'm…sorry for dragging you into it."

"It's a goblin-hunting scenario," Goblin Slayer replied evenly. "There is no problem."

It was nothing *but* problems. Under his steel helmet, Goblin Slayer's lips tugged upward.

In front of his eyes was a goblin horde. Behind him was the quest giver. He was injured and exhausted. He would soon reach his limit. The effect of a stamina potion was essentially an advance on your own vitality. Beyond that limit, there was no more strength.

By hook or by crook, if he could kill goblins, then it was no chore for him.

Ah yes, but…

What have I got in my pocket?

It was one of the riddles his master had asked him.

He never had figured out the answer. Perhaps it had been a ring of some sort.

But he did know what he had in *his* pocket at that moment.

"My hands."

It was ever thus.

It was not a question of able or unable, nor of whether things would go well or poorly.

It was only *do* or *do not*.

First, Goblin Slayer took the ax in his hand and threw it. It spun through the air, struck a goblin in the head handle first, then bounced off him and lodged its blade in the head of the goblin next to him.

"GOROOOOBB!"

"GGGB! GOOBG!"

The goblins howled and yammered. Goblin Slayer reached into his bag and drew out a certain item.

"I will buy us time."

And then, weaponless, he walked forward, into the maelstrom of goblins.

"GOOBOG!"

"GBBB! GBGO!"

Empty-handed fighting. The goblins laughed out loud to see him walk toward them, looking pathetic with his panoply of injuries. Arc Mage looked up with the distinct sense that the laughter was mocking her.

"Buy us time?"

The shapeless mist was in front of her.

Under her feet ran the blood of goblins, or of Goblin Slayer—she didn't know which.

If she turned around, she assumed she would find a sea of blood. But she didn't turn around.

"*I…am such…an idiot!*"

If you have no time, just buy some.

It was so simple! Why hadn't she considered that fact sooner?

Arc Mage gave the crimson pool under her foot a powerful tap.

She gave herself over to the flow of red magic that came welling up, putting her hand to her deck of cards, to the spell book she had compiled.

"You, lightning, follow after me—!"

One card torn in half. An incantation shouted.

The red bolt of lightning emerging beneath her feet flashed as if to bless what she willed. And on her finger, the spark shimmered.

"*Expedite!*"

Arc Mage accelerated, leaving the world behind. Her flesh, her thinking, her very mind. As a result, she didn't fully register what had happened until it was all over.

Goblins poured in from the entryway of the chamber. Pressing forward, coming close.

Goblin Slayer moved toward them, something grasped in his hand.

He thought he could hear the sound of dice rolling somewhere far away. He didn't like it at all.

He had no intention of trusting his quest giver's life to any such thing.

"GOBBGR!"

"GOR! GROOOBG!!"

The goblins crashed in like a surging wave— No. Goblin Slayer knew what a true wave was. He had never seen one, but he had learned about them.

"*Take this, you fiends!*"

An instant later, the scroll he had untied exploded stupendously.

No, it only appeared to explode.

It was in fact a geyser of water that blocked out vision. An overpowering stench of salt.

Goblin Slayer had never seen the ocean, but he had learned that this was how it smelled.

"GOOBOGR?!"

"GGO?! GOROG?!"

The goblins, though, had no way of knowing that. They didn't even have a moment to contemplate what had happened.

They would never have conceived that the water had come spewing out of the scroll held by the man in front of them.

The goblins screamed, their bodies torn apart by a rush of high-pressure seawater. Resistance was simply futile.

Goblin Slayer was confident that the water would fill the tower from top to bottom.

The plan he had thought of when Witch had told him about Gate scrolls worked beautifully. She had been in high spirits when he asked her for help, dubbing him "Most interesting."

"I agree," Goblin Slayer muttered, tossing aside the scroll as a supernatural flame consumed it and sitting down. "This is most interesting indeed."

§

He was greeted with a bizarre sight.

Goblin Slayer had never seen anything like it before; it looked like something that shouldn't exist in this world.

A four-sided crystal twisted in upon itself, writhing and projecting rays like tentacles. It appeared like a chaotic roil of bubbles, and when he looked directly at it, he couldn't pin down its shape—something phantasmal.

This was the six-hundred polychoron, as Arc Mage had called it. He didn't particularly understand the expression.

He did, however, understand that the door had been unlocked and opened, and that was all he needed to know.

"You do know how to pull a crazy stunt, don't you?" Arc Mage said as they pushed open the ebony door and began to climb slowly up a long golden spiral staircase. "A water attack? I wonder what you planned to do if the tower collapsed. Same question goes for a cave. You'd be buried alive."

"It was the first time I've tried it," he said defensively. "It was effective, but it wouldn't be versatile."

"No kidding." Arc Mage didn't sound very happy. "Can't go betting your life on an unreliable trump card."

One step, two steps, three. She almost seemed like she was about to start skipping up the stairs; she turned to face him in a spin that was nearly a twirl. The smell of cider drifted to him, and he stopped walking.

A finger was pointed directly at the visor of his helmet.

"By hook or by crook, if you can win, then it's never a chore."

"Yes." Goblin Slayer nodded. "I will be careful."

"Good." Arc Mage puffed out her chest, pleased, and nodded like an instructor. The two of them resumed walking.

The stairs seemed to go on forever—forever and ever. The only sounds were their footsteps and their breathing, and the lack of windows meant the dark inner wall wound upward, on and on.

They had no idea how high they were, nor what time it was. Most likely, dawn would be breaking soon. But now they were probably still in the last watches of the night. Goblin Slayer considered the matter idly. He couldn't say why he thought this. He just did.

Arc Mage and Goblin Slayer were both at the limits of their endurance. Their steps were unsteady, their vision wavered. Their breath came in short gasps. Their feet dragged like stones.

But for one reason or another, they took no rest. They only acknowledged the fact of their fatigue; the desire to take a break didn't enter into their minds.

They continued climbing the stairs, silently.

They kept climbing, so why did it feel as if they were traveling down the center of the spiral? Suddenly, Goblin Slayer thought he caught a heart-aching aroma of stew.

It had to be his imagination. A product of the exhaustion.

With that, he cast aside all his doubts.

And thus—not, perhaps, because of this, but all the same—the next thing he knew, there were no more steps to climb.

They had arrived at a landing, at the very top of the spiral staircase. In front of them was—of course—an ebony door.

"..." Arc Mage brushed her hand along it, almost a caress. It was designed like a double door, but there was no seam. "...I'm gonna open it, okay?"

Goblin Slayer nodded. Arc Mage placed her trembling palm against the door.

She didn't push very hard; the door seemed to open of its own accord, beckoning them inward. And then…

Fwoo. There was a breath of wind.

It was the sky.

Dark blue, then red, then white, the clear night sky.

Clouds drifted by, a pale blue color, a whole train of little wisps carried by the wind.

This very landing was the edge of the world. And so what was beyond must be that which was completely beyond.

Arc Mage looked at the door, the door to empty space, as if she might burst into tears at any moment…and smiled.

Ahh, so this is it. Or perhaps, *I finally made it.*

The difference between the two emotions was subtle, and Goblin Slayer couldn't decide which it was.

"Satisfied?"

"Yes, no." She blinked several times, then gently rubbed the corners of her eyes. "It's not quite over."

"I see."

"The place I want to go, it's past here. So I have to go on."

"I see," Goblin Slayer said again, then nodded and looked at the sky.

He had once climbed a snowy mountain with his master, and the view from the summit had looked much like this.

He remembered his master humming some sort of song. He didn't much understand poems or songs, so he had forgotten it—but now he wondered if it might have been good to remember it.

"Ahh, now I see… So that's the story." Arc Mage spoke suddenly, her voice small. She put a hand to her ample chest, took in a deep breath, and let it out. Spark glittered on her finger as it rose and fell in time with her breathing.

Then she looked at him with a smile as clear and soft as the sky itself.

She looked at *him*, under his helmet, hidden behind his visor.

"I'm sorry about all this. It looks like I've dragged you into my own scenario."

She had said the same thing to him before. So he answered the same way he had then.

"It's a goblin-hunting scenario, isn't it?"

So it is. And it had been, from the very beginning to the bitter end.

Goblin Slayer said calmly, "You talk too much, but you tell me what's important. There is no problem."

Arc Mage looked at him in surprise, then pursed her lips a little almost as if pouting. "You... You are truly a strange man."

"Is that so?"

"I should certainly think so."

"I see."

He nodded, and she let out a chuckle rather like the one she'd given when they first met, but somehow different.

"Say," Arc Mage said, looking at him curiously. "Do you know that old legend...the one about the giant who spent an eternity trying to scoop out the ocean with a shell?"

Goblin Slayer thought a moment before he answered. "No, I don't know it."

He had a vague sense he might have heard it once from his sister but found he couldn't quite remember.

There were so many things he had forgotten or didn't know. About his sister. About his master.

"What about it?"

"...The giant scooped all the way down to the bottom of the sea, where he found a rare treasure, a jewel beneath the waves. Or so they say."

"I see."

"That's why I won't laugh."

"..."

"I won't laugh if you become Goblin Slayer."

Goblin Slayer didn't say anything.

Arc Mage squinted as if she was satisfied with that, then reached out her hand to the sky, though she knew it couldn't touch what she desired.

On her finger, the ring flickered.

"I told you once. Your knowledge is a spark."

Sometimes a person goes through life without ever striking a spark.

Sometimes they go on some adventure, die in some deep, dark place, and that's the end for them.

The words seemed to pile up on her outstretched hand.

"But still, there's a spark." Just like so many of those who dare to become adventurers… "You have one, too."

So I won't laugh.

Goblin Slayer didn't immediately respond to her. He moved his helmet, looked at the sky. The sky, just streaked with the first hints of golden daybreak.

He didn't know what he ought to say, nor what he ought to do.

"…And what about yours?"

"My…?" When he finally produced a question, Arc Mage squinted against the brilliance of the sun and answered, "I don't know. That's what I'm going to find out." Then she slowly removed the Spark ring and held it out to Goblin Slayer. "On the way home… No, on the way forward, you'll need this, won't you?

"I'm leaving the rest up to you," she said, then winked awkwardly.

"Think of it as…your reward. In advance."

"My reward," Goblin Slayer murmured, eliciting a quiet "Uh-huh" from Arc Mage.

"For everything I've asked of you on this quest, and beyond."

"…"

"Ask the receptionist to fill you in on the details. You two are close, right?"

Were they? Goblin Slayer didn't know.

Was he, in fact, close to anyone?

Thus, he thought for a moment, then decided to ask about the only thing he needed to know.

"…Will it help me hunt goblins?"

"Personally, I hope so."

I see. Goblin Slayer nodded. Then he took the ring.

She said the Spark ring had the power of Breath. If he was going to keep drowning enemies—for that matter, even if he wasn't—it couldn't hurt to have it.

Whether anything would be of help, or not, was entirely his responsibility. That was what his master had taught him.

So he would make it useful. He decided on that then and there.

When she saw Goblin Slayer nod, she brushed his helmet with her now ringless hand.

"Well, see you."

And with those few words, she stepped out into the sky as casually as if she were walking out her front door.

Then she disappeared from Goblin Slayer's vision.

He waited and watched for a moment, but saw no sign that she would return.

He didn't know where she had gone, nor did he care. He assumed that no matter how carefully it was explained to him, he would never have understood.

She was not a party member. Nor had they adventured together.

If someone asked what she was to him, the answer was that they were quest giver and adventurer. Not friends, or anything else.

But perhaps, if pressed, he might have admitted that they had been what she had once called them.

Traveling companions.

Goblin Slayer looked in his hand. The ring glowed faintly. The shimmer of the Spark was fading as if it had never existed.

It was nothing more than a Breath ring now.

He stuffed it into his item pouch, then slowly started walking. He could hear the door close behind him, but he didn't even think of looking back.

When he began to attempt the long climb down the stairs, he found that the height was not so great, and he moved from floor to floor in almost no time at all.

But water had pooled here and there, goblin corpses floating in it.

Ah: indeed, he did need the ring.

He put it on his finger, and without hesitation, he dove into the water. He walked as if he were swimming, until he reached dry land, then he went under again and repeated the process.

In the blink of an eye, he had descended to the first floor. And when he emerged and looked back, the tower was vanishing like a shadow. The dawn sky seemed to go on forever as the sun emerged over the ridge of the mountains.

He squinted into the golden light and found he had a mysterious certainty that he would not see her again.

He went back to town, back to the Guild, and reported the quest complete, then stopped by the tavern. He ordered a mug of apple cider, which the chef silently handed to him, and which he drank in a single gulp before going back outside.

Beyond the crowded street, he could see the great, wide sky. He squinted behind his visor, holding the ring he'd received up to the light.

He could see there no glow of any spark.

She had said that one aspires to the summit because they want that place, they want the view, or they want whatever is beyond it. In that case...she must have wanted whatever was beyond this sky, whatever was past it.

He had no idea what might be out beyond the "board." No idea what she could have been seeking there.

A playing piece could hardly imagine the province of the players in heaven.

So maybe she had gone to uncover the truth of it all.

Maybe her aspiration had been to become a player herself.

That was as far as Goblin Slayer thought before slowly shaking his head back and forth.

It was far too presumptuous a thing for him to imagine. That had been her scenario, not his. He had been only a traveling companion, and in no position to judge the fruit of her labor.

Whatever trials they had overcome, whatever benefit they had received—it was all hers.

His stride was less certain now. Exhaustion weighed on every inch of him, and the cider had started to reach his brain.

Even so, his heart felt clear as the sky.

There was just one thing he could say with confidence.

She achieved what she wanted.

"Ngggaahhh!!"

Spearman tumbled away from the beak, letting out a sound that wasn't quite a scream but wasn't exactly a battle cry, either.

Rocks could be heard skittering across the pockmarked floor of the cave.

In front of Spearman as he regained his feet was a creature with a cruel glint in its eyes: a chicken.

But it had the wings of a bat, and the tail of a lizard. This was no ordinary creature.

"It's…a…cockatrice."

"Nobody told me about any bat-lizard-chickens…!"

Witch frowned in sympathy, but Spearman's exclamation was entirely understandable.

This was supposed to be an easy job—something one could practically do alone, never mind with a partner.

Needless to say, they'd made short work of the warlock when he'd shuffled out of his cave come nightfall. Witch had cast a spell of silence, preventing their opponent from uttering the words of his magic, and Spearman had given him one good stab through the heart.

When they pulled back his hood, they discovered that he was indeed one of the Non-Prayers. The seal of the evil sect hung at his chest.

And that had been that. All that remained was to search the cave, and then it was quest complete. Not without risk, but still, a one-night job. That was the idea anyway.

"When they told me 'easy work' always means 'dangerous work,' I should've listened...!"

Spearman, thinking back on some old lesson, heaped abuse on his past self. It had never crossed his mind that the warlock might be keeping a cockatrice as a guard dog.

"Just imagine if they started mass-producing these things... It'd be a nightmare...!"

He wanted to give the what for to himself for having come rushing headlong into this cave.

"...My spells... I have just, one more," Witch said from behind him, her voice low and calm.

It would have been much better to try this after they had rested for a night—not in any suggestive sense, mind you, but purely to restore Witch's magic.

Stupid, stupid, stupid, stupid, stupid, he thought, but no matter how much he upbraided himself, the situation didn't change. Spearman glared at the cockatrice as it scratched the ground violently, then he dropped into a deep stance.

"If it keeps its distance, I think we can manage somehow. But if it comes charging in, we're done for..."

"..." He could hear Witch gulp behind him. "...You, think, you... can, manage?"

"If it doesn't charge. That's the trick."

"I'll try," Witch said nervously. Spearman trusted her. He was loath to run, even if it cost him his life.

Gotta look good for the lady, after all!

"Zrrraaahhhh!!" The cockatrice made a birdlike yet unearthly noise, and Spearman responded by dropping his body even lower.

Witch's delicate lips spoke out words as if in a melody. *"Aranea... facio...ligator!* Spider, come and bind!"

It was the work of an instant.

Spearman charged. The cockatrice kicked the ground and attempted to take flight, but its leg was trapped.

Caught in a spiderweb.

Spearman hadn't seen it, hadn't even really thought about it; he just knew it intuitively.

A sticky, milky something was wrapped around the monster's feet. *Perfect!*

All he needed now was one turn to finish things. He hefted his spear and drove it into the cockatrice's heart with all his strength.

Killing an immobilized chicken is easier than shooting fish in a barrel.

"Excellent, and now to find the loot!"

"Yes, indeed…" Witch nodded, appearing detached as usual, but her eyes glinted with curiosity.

Such was the spice of adventuring. Hack your way in, slash your way out. And when it came to a warlock's base of operations, you could expect to find a considerable reward.

It didn't take them long to find a treasure chest. They spent a moment looking it over, trying to ascertain whether it was booby-trapped and wishing they had a scout.

"…Okay, here goes."

"…Mn."

He saw Witch nod, then had her back away from the chest—just in case—and broke the seal.

Inside was a long, thin pole apparently made from some kind of wood. There was a decorated metal tip on one end, and it glittered with magical power.

"Ohh…!" Spearman's eyes opened wide, and in an excess of joy he grabbed the item. "A spear…!"

A magical weapon. Any warrior worth his salt would lust after one. There were all kinds, from those that just boasted a little extra cutting power, or never rusted, to the weapons of legend. There was no one, from the most rustic country runaway to the most experienced knight, who didn't occasionally dream of them.

But then Witch, peeking from beside him, gave a regretful shake of her head. "…This is…a staff, believe me."

"…You're kidding."

"*No,*" she replied in a strained, apologetic voice. "*This is a wizard's staff.*"

Brushing the metal tip—the one Spearman had taken for a spear point—gently, Witch took the staff in hand.

"But…if, we…sell, it…it will…bring in some…money."

"Huh?" Spearman looked at her like she was crazy. "Why would we sell it?"

"…?" Now it was Witch's turn to look mystified. "We, agreed…to split, the reward, no?"

Spearman scratched his head. Then he sighed: this was common sense.

"When you party up, you focus on building your total fighting strength. You use it.

"But if you don't want it, then we can sell it," he added, closing the lid of the empty treasure chest.

Witch stood holding the staff in her hands. She looked speechless, like a child who's been told they can have anything they want.

"…You're, right," she finally said, and with the staff still gripped in one hand, she gave the brim of her hat a sharp tug. "Then, until we find…a magic spear, I'll…borrow this. Okay?"

"It ain't a loan," Spearman said, punching her gently in the shoulder. It was an immensely casual, spur of the moment gesture. "Call it an investment in the future."

Witch slowly smiled.

Her smile looked like a flower coming into bloom.

CHAPTER 6

AFTER SESSION, SCENARIO HOOK
The Reward and the Next Adventure

Creak, creak. Even empty, the cart's wheels complained as they rolled along the road.

Cow Girl walked with her hands folded behind her, watching him as he pulled the cart.

He said he wanted some help, but...

He hadn't said with what, or where. Not a word. It left her wondering if she should have agreed so readily. Maybe her uncle was right to worry about her.

If I asked, he would tell me...

Or so that woman had suggested to her, but that required working up the courage to ask.

Even just walking a step behind him took its own sort of bravery. Walking placidly along was just evidence of a baseless conviction that the ground would be there to meet her feet.

One had to have that faith, though, or one would never be able to move. She vaguely recalled laughing about something like that in the past.

His back as he walked silently along seemed so close to her, yet somehow so far away, and Cow Girl cast her eyes up to the sky as if to escape it.

It was so blue. A summer sky, blue and white enough to make her catch her breath.

Far up in the azure expanse, a single bird, a hawk, circled slowly.

It was unusual, she thought. She had never seen a hawk fly this far before. She dimly remembered that hawks preferred the mountains.

Maybe she had just never noticed. How often in her life had she just gazed up at the sky?

The sky was always there, and yet, she so rarely looked hard at it. It was strange.

"Huh…?"

She suddenly noticed that he was heading not toward town, but toward the outskirts. She hurried to close the gap that had opened between them, and with restraint, but also evident concern, she asked, "We aren't…going to town?"

"No."

That hesitant step she had dared to take was met with solid ground underfoot. She let out a relieved breath.

"But we need the cart?"

"Yes."

The second step, safe. She felt like she was clinging to a vine on the side of a sheer cliff.

Not that I would know what that actually feels like…

Cow Girl giggled to herself. If either of them was likely to wind up in that situation, it would be him.

A short time later, he stopped.

They had come to an old shed on the riverside, a place that looked like it had been there for who knew how long. The morning sun shone down on it, but it seemed strangely lifeless and silent. The creaking waterwheel was broken, and no smoke came from the chimney. A hovel. It felt almost as if this place and this place alone had been torn out of a picture.

He thought for a moment, then walked up to the door, giving the brass knocker a few solid, casual strikes. He waited, but there was no reply, so he opened the door and walked into the gloomy interior.

Books clogged even the front entranceway; he wove his way among them through the room.

Cow Girl stood at the door, not quite sure what to do, but finally, she resolved herself and spoke up.

The third step.

"…Is this it?"

"It is."

"Don't mind me," Cow Girl said hesitantly, then took a careful step inside.

The inside—how to describe it?

It was like a condemned building, an abandoned house… Or a wizard's home.

At first glance, everything seemed strange and incomprehensible, herbs and medicines packed everywhere. There was nowhere to step—it was enough to make her wonder if they'd wandered into a warehouse.

He walked among the detritus confidently, a sign he had been here many times before. Cow Girl did her best to follow him, taking care not to catch her clothing on anything.

She survived the trip, and they emerged into an open space in the middle of it all. There sat a desk and a chair, looking untouched for some mystifying reason.

There were empty bottles scattered around near the furniture.

He glanced at the desk, the chair, and the bottles. Then he shook his head.

"I will take some things from here," he said quietly. "What I need."

"Is that okay?" Cow Girl asked, to which he replied only, "It is my reward."

Thus, the fourth step.

Cow Girl helped him, reluctantly ferrying strange magical items outside.

She had never seen so many books in one place. For an instant, she considered trying to read them, but they looked expensive, so she thought better of it.

The books, piled all over the floor instead of on bookshelves, were covered in dust; she blew a sharp breath over the one she held in her hands. She didn't know how best to take care of books, but this one smelled a little musty, so maybe it ought to be dried out.

"What are you going to do with these?"

To her fifth question, he answered, "I will have the Guild donate them to the temple of the God of Knowledge or the like. Then those who need them can read them."

"That sounds like a good idea," she said, trying to check that she was about to put her foot in a safe place. "I'm sure it'll help. I mean, books are full of all sorts of things, aren't they?"

"…" He nodded, and then replied, "Yes."

All morning, Cow Girl had been thinking how glad she was that she came here.

The cramped room was ostentatiously crowded with detritus. Just removing it all was serious work. Organizing it was another major task. And loading it onto the cart, still another.

By the time they were finished, the sun was past its apex, and Cow Girl was breathing hard and wiping the sweat from her brow.

"Wow! I guess we've missed lunch already…" Fatigue was one thing, but a long history of hard work had left her well able to endure an empty stomach. She calmly rubbed a hand on her abdomen. How was he doing? She cocked her head. "I should have packed lunches for us or something."

"I see."

She had spoken so quietly, the words directed only at herself, that she was startled to hear him answer her. She opened her mouth to say *That's not what I meant*, and then she realized that he was looking her way beneath his metal helmet. And when she realized it, she gulped.

"I am sorry about that."

"N-no, don't worry…"

The sixth step she hadn't realized she was taking met also with solid ground—or anyway, so she felt.

Taken aback, Cow Girl moved her hand from her belly to her chest. She half-hugged herself.

"…If you ask, I'll make one for you, okay?"

"Understood."

Pushing the cart, the two of them set off walking.

"What should we do?" she asked, and he answered, "First, I will deliver the books to the Guild."

When they passed through the town gate, nearby adventurers would glance at them and then look away again. It was as if, although they were doing something strange, people refused to notice them. Cow Girl wasn't thrilled others thought of them that way, but for some reason, it didn't bother her that much.

I wonder why not.

Strangely, she herself wasn't sure. But it wasn't a bad feeling.

Finally, they arrived at the Adventurers Guild, and he put the cart where it would be out of the way.

"I will go report to reception that I am finished," he said. Then his helmet tilted thoughtfully, and in a slow, confirmatory tone, he said, "You are free to eat at the tavern."

Rather than pleasing, Cow Girl found this oddly funny, and she giggled. "That's okay," she said, and then, worried that her meaning wasn't getting through, she added, "Let's eat at home, together, okay?"

He fell silent.

Cow Girl felt as if, in her exuberance, she had taken a step too far.

But then he said quietly, "I see."

His response was the same two words as ever, but to her they were meaningful. "I'm glad you do."

"Is that so?"

Yeah, sure is. Then she repeated to herself: *It sure is.* He nodded.

"In that case, I will return shortly."

"Sure."

And then Cow Girl watched him as he disappeared into the Guild building.

She could see a smile light up Guild Girl's face as he came through the swinging doors.

Cow Girl sat on the cart bed, feeling strangely floaty. She rested her elbows on her knees and her chin in her hands. She let her legs hang down and looked at the town. Gaggles of adventurers coming and going. Townspeople of every sort. Just the usual scenery.

But it was just like the sky. How many times had she really looked closely at it?

Without a doubt, there were at least a few people around here eating things that came from her farm. The thought gave her a little rush of happiness. It made her feel that even just helping her uncle with his chores had some kind of meaning.

Suddenly, Cow Girl heard a breathy voice.

"Well, now…?"

Lost in her thoughts, she hadn't noticed the voice's owner approaching her.

"It's been…some, time."

"Oh!" Cow Girl stood up quickly. It was that beautiful woman, the witch. "Yes, it's been a while!" She hopped down off the cart and bowed. The movement was so sudden, it all came off a little more energetically than she'd intended. Embarrassed, she blushed, and a chuckle rolled from somewhere deep in Witch's throat.

"What…brings…you here, today…?"

"Oh, uh…" Cow Girl looked into thin air for an answer. "I'm helping… Helping him."

We brought this to the Guild.

Witch squinted at that and caressed the books piled on the cart. "Ah…"

"I don't know much about them myself. But I guess they're valuable, right?"

"Yes, indeed… For those, who…want them."

To those people, they are valuable. Witch whispered, then her cheeks twitched in a smile.

Huh? Cow Girl just sensed something, cocked her head in curiosity. Could it be? Just maybe?

"…Having a good day yourself?"

"Heh, heh." Witch blinked, her long eyelashes wavering. Her lips moved ever so slightly, as if chanting the words of some secret spell. "I, will…be going…on, a 'date.'"

"Wow," Cow Girl breathed, and Witch covered her mouth with her hand as if shy about the way she began to giggle.

"See, you."

With a languid wave, she walked away, hips swaying. In the distance was a spear-wielding adventurer.

Lucky woman…

Although Cow Girl had to admit she didn't fully grasp why she thought Witch was lucky.

"I'm finished."

"Oh, okay."

They left, and he returned. Cow Girl nodded and went around behind the cart.

She started unloading books. He grabbed piles of them himself and set them down.

"So where are they going to donate these to?"

"I don't know," he said bluntly. "They said they would keep the books here and look into it, then decide."

"*Huh*," she said. "*Yes*," he said.

Cow Girl piled up the books, hauled them off the cart, and gave them to a Guild staff member. Then she did it again.

Just then, though, she thought she caught a whiff of some sweet scent.

The aroma of apples. At least, that's what she thought it was.

So she stopped and took a deep breath, wiping the sweat from her forehead, and without really thinking about it, she asked a question.

"I haven't seen that woman around lately, huh?"

He stopped moving. Was something wrong? Cow Girl cocked her head, and the steel helmet moved.

"Who do you mean?" he asked

"You know, the one you were working with." Cow Girl looked up at the sky, almost unsure what she was saying. It was so blue it hurt her eyes. "…The wizard."

He didn't reply immediately. He piled up several books, brought them down, handed them to the staff member, then piled up more books, removed them, and handed them over as well.

Cow Girl waited patiently. She had taken so many steps already. She was sure this one would be safe.

When his reply came at last, it was tremendously vague and all too brief. "I think she went somewhere far away. She may not be coming home."

Cow Girl replied simply, "Is that right?"

She imagined the worst, but somehow hesitated to give the idea voice.

When he saw she had gone silent, he stopped working. And then, in a startlingly gentle tone, he said, "I do not believe she is dead."

At that moment—if she wasn't simply mistaken—she would have sworn she heard him laugh ever so softly.

She felt some relief at that and let out a breath. Not dead. That was wonderful.

Still unsure herself why she had asked about the woman, she went on to her next words. "Do you miss her?"

"I don't know."

His answer was brief.

When he had piled up and taken away the last book, he finally let out a breath. Then, the helmet still on his head, he looked at the ground, deep in thought, and finally shook his head from side to side. "I don't know, but…in a way, perhaps I do."

"I see," Cow Girl said, and then she whispered again, "I see," and wiped away sweat.

They entrusted the last of the books to the Guild staff, and then the two of them set off on the road home.

He pulled the cart as they walked the path back to the farm, which seemed so long and yet so short.

In fact, there was still quite a load on the cart. It was her job to push it from behind.

"…Wanna switch places?"

"No," he said as he pulled on the crossbeam. "This is my job."

"Oh yeah?"

"I think so."

Then there was no more conversation, and the two of them focused on walking silently along.

On the road, they passed adventurers wearing every imaginable type of equipment. A young girl with her silver hair tied up went running by, followed by her party, and then a young warrior.

A spear-wielding adventurer walked along, looking intimidating and important, accompanied by a witch holding an ancient-looking staff with great care.

He and Cow Girl went slowly in the opposite direction, one step at a time.

The sun had bent low in the sky by now, and the road back to the farm, though it wasn't long, was dyed a deep red.

How many years had it been since they last walked a road like this together?

Come to think of it...

Something like that had happened. A memory so small she had hardly recalled it until this moment.

I remember playing jump rope together.

A children's song she hadn't sung in ages came back to her lips.

Gods, Gods!
Roll the dice and play a game.
Roll a one and I'll comfort you,
roll a two and I'll laugh with you,
roll a three and I'll praise you,
roll a four and I'll give you a treat,
roll a five and I'll dance for you,
roll a six and I'll kiss you,
roll a seven and...

"Roll a seven and...?"

It took her a second to realize the laconic voice was his.

"Roll a seven and then what?"

Cow Girl looked shyly at the ground—even though he couldn't see her—and laughed. "...I guess I don't remember."

"I see."

"It's kind of a weird song, huh? Dice only have six sides."

You could roll two dice, but then you couldn't get a one.

Her murmur was almost a way to change the subject, but he only replied, "You're right."

She stole a glance at him; he seemed to be simply gazing up at the sky as he pulled the cart along.

"____"

For some reason, the sight of him made Cow Girl think of the farm fence that had been repaired.

Yeah, that makes sense.

She hadn't realized at the time. Why had it caught her attention?

She'd originally thought her uncle had done it. But she had seen plenty of her uncle's work around and was used to it. She rarely noticed it at all as such.

The young man awkwardly shaving wood splinters away, striving to finish something by twilight.

Had it been some toy? A wooden sword? Something else? Her memory was hazy now. But the familiar image came back to her, and she squinted her eyes and laughed.

For some reason, the sunset looked terribly blurry. The cargo piled on the cart clattered and shifted as the wheels ran over rocks on the road.

All the stuff on the cart was junk Cow Girl couldn't really identify, but he said he was going to put it in his shed. It would take till nightfall, she assumed. And she would help him.

If that empty outbuilding were to hold even a few of his own possessions in it, she thought that would be a very good thing.

If they worked until nightfall, they would certainly be hungry. They would need to eat.

She would warm up some stew, and then she and he and her uncle could all eat together.

That struck her as an excellent idea.

"Okay, then," she said, putting extra strength into pushing the cart along. "When we do my jobs, then I get to pull."

And you help. He was silent for a moment, but then replied, "Understood."

"Uh-huh." She nodded and gave another shove.

The farm was just ahead.

AFTERWORD

Hullo! Kumo Kagyu here.

Did you enjoy *Goblin Slayer: Year One*, Vol. 2?

Maybe it feels a bit like *Year Two* or *The Long Halloween*.

So would that make Volume 3 *Dark Victory*? It's a riddle.

In any event, this was another story in which goblins appeared, and so Goblin Slayer slayed them.

That's everything that matters to him, it's all he can see, so it's all he does.

It's not as if he didn't meet anyone in this volume, but living is difficult, isn't it?

One step at a time, we'll eventually arrive at the main series, but the road to get there is long.

In other words, this is what "experience points" are like... That's what I'm thinking.

I tried my best to write a story that evoked that sort of feeling, and if you enjoyed it, that would make me very happy.

Once again, I was only able to complete this work thanks to the help of many different people:

To my gaming buddies and creative friends, thank you very much as always.

To Shingo Adachi, who handled the illustrations. Thank you for designing "Arc-san"!

To Kento Sakaeda, who does the manga adaptation—we've just reached the climax of Volume 1, and it's incredible!

To all the admins of all the summary blogs, thank you so much for your continuing encouragement.

I didn't exactly grow up to be an astronaut, but I've done my utmost to bring pride to my hometown.

To everyone in the editorial division, thank you as ever for all your help. I owe you a lot—again.

To all the people I've never met but who were crucial in producing and working with this book, thank you very much.

I know the series is called *Year One*, but if I get an opportunity, I'd love to go on and do a third volume. I'm sure it will also entail goblins whom Goblin Slayer has to slay.

If that book ever does come out, I hope you'll pick it up.

Till next time.

HE DOES NOT LET ANYONE ROLL THE DICE.

A young Priestess joins her first adventuring party, but blind to the dangers, they almost immediately find themselves in trouble. It's Goblin Slayer who comes to their rescue—a man who has dedicated his life to the extermination of all goblins by any means necessary. A dangerous, dirty, and thankless job, but he does it better than anyone. And when rumors of his feats begin to circulate, there's no telling who might come calling next...

Light Novel V. 1-2 Available Now!

Check out the simul-pub manga chapters every month!

Yen Press   Yen ON
www.yenpress.com